Agents of Dreamland

ALSO BY CAITLÍN R. KIERNAN

AGENTS of DREAMLAND

CAITLÍN R. KIERNAN

A TOM DOHERTY ASSOCIATES BOOK

NEW YORK

This is a work of fiction. All of the characters, organizations, and events portrayed in this novella are either products of the author's imagination or are used fictitiously.

AGENTS OF DREAMLAND

Cover photograph © Getty Images
Cover design by Christine Foltzer

Edited by Jonathan Strahan

A Tor.com Book
Published by Tom Doherty Associates
175 Fifth Avenue
New York, NY 10010

www.tor.com

Tor® is a registered trademark of
Macmillan Publishing Group, LLC.

ISBN 978-0-7653-9431-6 (ebook)
ISBN 978-0-7653-9432-3 (trade paperback)

First Edition: February 2017

For Kathryn

Eventually you've got to understand that
an answer isn't the same thing as a solution,
and a story is sometimes only an excuse.

—**Nic Pizzolatto**

Agents of Dreamland

1.

Oddfellows Local 171
(July 9, 2015)

HERE'S THE SCENE: It's Thursday evening, and the Signalman sits smoking and nursing a flat Diet Dr Pepper, allowing himself to breathe a stingy sigh of relief as twilight finally, mercifully comes crashing down on the desert. The heavens above West Second Street are blazing like it's 1945 all over again and the Manhattan Project has mistakenly triggered the Trinity blast one state over from the White Sands Proving Ground. Or, he thinks, like this is the moment fifty thousand years ago when a huge nickel-iron meteorite vaporized herds of mastodons, horses, and giant ground sloths just sixteen miles southwest of this shitty little diner and its cracked Naugahyde seats and flyblown windows. Either simile works just fine by the Signalman; either way, the sky's falling. Either way is entirely apropos. He checks his wristwatch again, sees that it's been only seven minutes since the last time, then goes back to staring out the plate glass as shadows and fire vie for control of the dingy, sunbaked soul of Winslow, Arizona. His unkind face stares at him from the glass, easily ten years older than the date on his birth certificate. He curses, stubs out his cigarette, and lights another.

It's not that she's late. It's that the train from L.A. dumped him out in this den of scorpions and Navajo tchotchkes at 6:39 A.M., and by 7:15 A.M., whatever wasteland charm the town might hold had worn thin and worn out. What the fuck do you say about a place whose sole claim to fame is a mention in an Eagles song? He got a room at La Posada, the celebrated Mary Colter masterpiece of terra-cotta and stucco, but then discovered that he couldn't sleep. He turned on the radio and tried to read a book he'd brought, but it was impossible to concentrate; he kept reading the same paragraphs over again. So the Signalman spent the day haunting the sidewalks—restless, sweating, half blind from the sun, wearing down the heels of his JCPenney oxfords, and ocasionally ducking in somewhere for a soda, then ducking out again into the heat. Wanting to be drunk, needing to stay sober. The scalding air stank of dust and creosote, and he watched the local PD watching him, their minds clicking like locusts. *Who is this scarecrow in a cheap suit and Wayfarers that the* Southwest Chief *has seen fit to disgorge on our doorstep?* If it weren't for the long arm of the

Company, he'd likely have been arrested for loitering or vagrancy—or something else. But all his papers are in order, copacetic, so to speak, no matter how off the books and need to know this meet-up might be. Albany isn't taking chances, not tonight. Not when Y has seen fit to cough up the likes of Immacolata Sexton for a sit-down.

The waitress comes around again and asks if he needs anything else, a refill or maybe a piece of pie. There's lemon meringue, she tells him. There's blueberry. He would say she's a pretty enough girl, despite the ugly scar over her left eye, a pretty girl who's escaped the hillside slums of Heroica Nogales to serve cheeseburgers and huevos rancheros in this gringo grease trap. Still, it's a job, right? Better than her mother ever had, a woman who died at forty-three after twenty-five years sewing designer tags on jeans in a maquiladora. The Signalman knows the waitress' story, just as he knows the stories of the two cooks and the dishwasher, just as he knows the names of the proprietor's three daughters. Every little thing that the Signalman *doesn't* know is a blind spot, a weakness he can't afford and won't abide.

"Estoy bien, gracias," he says, but doesn't ask for the check. On her way back to the counter, she glances over her shoulder, and he catches the glint of wariness in her eyes.

The Signalman checks his watch again.

And then the brass cowbell nailed above the diner door jingles, and he looks up as a tall, pale woman steps in off the street. She's carrying a carbon-fiber Zero Halliburton attaché case in her left hand. For a moment, it seems to him like something is trailing behind her, as if the coming night has tangled itself about her shoulders, has snagged in her short black hair and won't let go. But the impression passes, and he sits up a little straighter in the booth, tugs nervously at his tie, and nods to her. The Signalman's heard stories enough to fill a fat paperback bestseller, but he never expected to actually meet this woman face-to-face. Immacolata Sexton is a long way from home.

She takes off her sunglasses, and he wishes that she hadn't.

"They have pie," he tells her as she settles into the seat across from him. "Lemon meringue. And blueberry, too. Welcome to Winslow."

One of his jobs is not to flinch. It's right there in the fine print.

"I didn't see you at first," she says. "I thought maybe I'd been stood up." She has a hint of a Southern Appalachian accent—North Alabama or East Tennessee—and a funny way of moving her lips, so that they hardly seem to move at all. It's a little like watching a ventriloquist at work.

"Has that ever actually happened?" he asks, stubbing out his cigarette, only half smoked, in the saucer he's been using for an ashtray.

"On occasion," she replies, "but never by the same person twice." She points at the saucer and the cigarette butts. "You can smoke in here?"

"No one's told me not to, and I don't see any signs posted. I took that as a yes."

The waitress comes back, and the Signalman knows that whatever she sees when *she* stares into the eyes of the operative from Y, it's not what *he* sees. Civilians get all the breaks. Immacolata orders coffee.

"I will admit," she says when the waitress has gone, "I was skeptical when I heard they'd assigned you to the case. After Maine and all. Rumor has it, an awful lot of the blame for that mess landed squarely at your feet. They say it was you who waited so long to take the situation seriously, that you were the man who ignored the writing on the wall."

"Rumor," he says. "Is that what passes for intel at Barbican Estate these days?"

She shrugs and lights a Marlboro; the smoke curls about her face. "Well," she says, "it's what I heard, that's all."

Of course she's leading off with Maine. A sharp left hook and all that, get him off-balance and reeling right from the start. As if just the sight of her weren't more than enough for that. Sure, he's got his own headful of rumors to go with that face she wears, but the Signalman knows better than to start trotting them out. He knows better than to ask any one of the dozen questions darting about behind his eyes.

Is it true what they say about your mother?

About your father?

About Berlin and the night the Wall came down?

He rubs his eyes and turns his head back towards the wide diner window and the last smoldering dregs of sunset. Across the street, outside a defunct and shuttered movie house, there are two guards standing watch like rejects from an episode of *The Man from U.N.C.L.E.* Her guards, even though the deal was they each come alone, no entourage, no backup, no fucking fan club, and he's honored his end of the bargain. But fuck it. There's no profit in making a fuss, not at this late date. He's here, she's here, and the only way out, kiddo, is straight on till morning. The waitress from Heroica Nogales is back at the table, talking to Immacolata, serving her coffee, and he counts off the interminable seconds until they're alone again.

"You can't be too careful," she says, stirring a packet of Sweet'n Low into her cup. The spoon clinks loudly against the china.

Is it true what they say about the night you were born?

"So, how was the trip up from Los Angeles?" she asks. "It's been a long time since I went anywhere by train."

"Forgive me, Ms. Sexton," he says, and fishes the last cigarette from the crumpled pack of Camel Wides he bought at noon. "I've never been particularly good with chitchat. Nothing personal, it's just—"

"Relax," she says, and he could swear her voice drips honey. "We're on the same side, aren't we? United by a common cause?"

What big eyes you have.

"Comrades-in-arms?"

"That's what they tell me," he mutters around the filter as he lights his cigarette. The Signalman takes a deep drag and holds the smoke until his ears start to hum.

"Right, well, I brought everything we have on Standish," she says, her demeanor changing entirely between one breath and the next, the strange creature that poured in off the cooling summer sidewalks of Winslow becoming suddenly businesslike and to the point, effortlessly shedding one mask and donning another. "We've had a million diligent monkeys with a million file cabinets hard at work ever since Barbican gave the thumbs-up last week. So, you go first. Show me yours, then I'll show you mine."

My, what big ears you have.

He hesitates only a few seconds before reaching into his suit jacket and taking out a brown kraft envelope, six inches by nine, stained with perspiration, creased down the middle, and bent at the edges. "Sorry," he says, "if mine's not quite as big as yours, but there's a shortage of monkeys—"

"—in Hollywood?" She smirks. "You expect me to believe that?"

The Signalman surrenders a halfhearted smile and opens the envelope, spreading the contents out on the table between them. Ten glossy black-and-white photographs, a tarot card, a flash drive, and a very old gold coin. At first glance, the photos could be shots from any murder scene, snapped by any forensic shutterbug. But only at first glance. Immacolata looks at him, and then she crushes out her Marlboro in the ersatz ashtray and picks up one of the pictures. She turns it over and briefly examines the back, where a date, time, and case number have been scribbled in indelible red ink, along with several Enochian symbols, and then she exchanges it for the tarot card.

"The World," she says. "The dancer is meant to signify the final attainment of man, a merging of the self-conscious with the unconscious and a blending of those two states with the superconscious. The World implies the ultimate state of cosmic awareness, the final goal to which all the other cards—of the Major Arcana, that is—have led. *Der Übergeist.*"

"I seriously fucking hope you've got something more for me than what we could pull off the Internet."

"You're an impatient man," she tells him.

"We're all on the clock with this one," he replies. "*New Horizons* makes its closest approach to Pluto five days from now. So, you'll excuse my sense of urgency, thank you and pretty please."

Immacolata lays the card back on the table, facedown, and selects another of the photographs. It strikes him for the first time how long and delicate her fingers are; they seem almost frail enough to snap like twigs.

Maybe they would. Maybe one day I'll get to find out.

"Jesus," Immacolata whispers, and she licks her ashen lips.

What big teeth you have.

The Signalman picks up one of the photographs, the one with his shadow in frame, the one where some trick of the light makes a corpse appear to be smiling. Every time he looks at these, every time he touches them, he feels unclean. He went through decon with the rest of the response team, but he only has to revisit these souvenirs of a horror show to be reminded how some stains sink straight through to the soul and are never coming out.

"How tight is the lid on this?" Immacolata asks him,

and she raises an eyebrow plucked straight and thin as a paper cut.

"It's all right there on the suicide drive," he tells her, and points at the contents of the envelope scattered across the Formica tabletop.

"No," she says. "I'm not asking you to parrot back to me what they've put in the reports. I didn't come here to play Polly Want a Cracker."

The Signalman stares at the tip of his cigarette, wishing this were going down in a proper fucking bar, someplace he could get a shot of Johnnie Walker Black or J&B. His mouth is as dry as the arroyos and sage waiting out there just beyond the halogen glare of the streetlights.

"We got lucky, after a fashion," he says. "We have geography on our side, the hot zone being situated where it is."

"That's not what I asked you," she protests.

"You ever been to the Salton Sea, Ms. Sexton? The lid's on fucking tight, okay? The CDC would get a hard-on, the lid's so goddamn tight. Neiman Marcus would be proud of our fucking window dressing."

He hears the annoyance in his voice, the aluminum-foil edge, and it pisses him off that she's getting to him.

"Am I making you nervous?"

No way in hell he's going to answer that question, not for a gold-plated penny.

"The Moonlight Ranch is about three miles north of Bombay Beach," he says instead. "Off Route 111. The only way in or out is a dirt road, not much more than a cattle trace. Lockdown is solid."

"The Moonlight Ranch? What, is that one of Watertown's supersecret code names?" And there's that smirk again, curling at the corners of her mouth and setting her eyes to glimmering.

I'd give a hundred bucks for a shot of rye whiskey, he thinks, and swallows hard. *I'd give a million to blow her fucking brains out.*

"No, that's just what the locals call it, and what Standish's followers called it."

"Yes, well, I'm beginning to have Helter Skelter flashbacks to Charlie Manson," she says. "Moonlight Ranch, the Spahn Movie Ranch, appropriate names for pens to hold all the thunderstruck little sheeple. We'll run cross-references, see what pops. You know we're expecting access to the quarantine zone, right?"

"Albany anticipated as much. You've got eyes-only clearance, and you've already been assigned a handler."

Immacolata nods, then leans back in the booth and just stares at that one photo held in her alabaster fingers. He's not even sure which one it is. The way she's holding it, he can't make out the number printed on the back.

"And you've got mycologists on the ground?" she

asks, then takes a sip of her coffee.

Moses on a motorbike, but isn't she cool enough to freeze brimstone in Hell? Wouldn't winding up on her bad side make a death sentence seem charitable?

"Yeah, sure. We've brought in people from Duke and the University of Michigan, and we've given them a state-of-the-art lab on the premises. Right now, they're talking about cutaneous and subcutaneous mycoses, hyperparasites, opportunistic pathogens, cryptococcosis, aspergillosis, entomopathogenic fungi, and fucking zombie ants," he tells Immacolata Sexton, reeling off remembered bits from Wednesday morning's briefings, not because he's trying to impress Y's asset, just because it's something to say, all that geek chatter. And, right now, saying anything feels better than saying nothing. "Jesus, you ever even heard of fucking zombie ants?"

She ignores the question, and he continues.

"But they've never seen shit like this, right. And you don't need a shrink to see it's sorta blowing their minds."

She nods and says, "I trust no one's been so careless as to whisper a word about Vermont or the Scituate Reservoir?" she asks without taking her eyes off the photograph.

"Despite what you may think, we're not total fucking idiots. Besides, it's not like they'll be walking away from this with their recollections intact."

"Perish the thought," she says, peeking at him over the top of the photo, and she taps the side of her nose three times.

"Anyway, that's what I brought, and I believe it's now your turn," says the Signalman, and he jabs a callused thumb at the attaché case. She nods and lays the picture from Moonlight Ranch back down on the table.

2.

Words Written Backwards
(June 29, 2015)

DREW IS TALKING TO ME, whispering in my ear, even though he's not here. At high noon I'm standing in the darkness cast by my own shadow—the only darkness remaining in the world—and I stare out across the desert, past Salt Creek, towards the hazy, uneven gray-periwinkle line that the Chocolate Mountains draw between the sky and the everlasting brownness of Coachella hardscrabble. *Behold, the Kingdom of Caliche and Horned Toads,* Drew said (and he laughed) the first day I was an inhabitant vomited upon the coast of the Sea. That day when first I stood upon the hot tin and followed the weathervane of his crooked finger. From there—from *here*—my eyes set eastward, I can see all the way to those crumbling schist ridges and peaks, laid down in Precambrian oceans. If I squint hard, man, and harder still, like I've been taught, I might as well be seeing much farther away, past what mere eyes can discern, to other mountain ranges and maybe all the way to the Palo Verde Valley and Blythe, where the desert is tormented so that green things will grow to feed us all and please the fickle eye of mankind. There are trees in Blythe. I remember trees.

Drew has gone away today on business, and Madeline went with him, and I am left here alone with myself and the others and with the sizzle of my brains in this woman's skull, a resonant frequency that perfectly matches white noise, the random signal possessed of a perpetual power supply, and in discrete time, a procession of serially uncorrelated random variables (finite variance, zero mean). These thoughts tumble on whirring insect wings in the hexagonal honeycomb of my mind's single eye, hollowing me out, while the sun chars me the same earth-tone shades as the desert. Down behind the husks of expired cars and trucks that make a rusty garden outside the ranch, the digital thermometer says it's 103.7 degrees F. We're having a cold snap. Up here, scraping myself against the belly of the sky, it must be so much hotter. But salvation has sailed me out beyond all fears of conflagration.

"It's so close now," Drew told us all last night. "You really have no notion how delightful it will be. Cross my heart and hope to die. Bo and Peep, Doe and Ti, as you are the Children of the Next Level."

His voice soothes the meat and mud of my soul.

"I believe we're the purest communists there are," says he. "Translation, evolution, metamorphosis, bliss in ever-lasting ice and trans-Neptunian, Kuiper Belt blackness, and you eat of *my* body, and we will traipse the light fantastic across aether wastes to be free of false Christs."

I don't know what half of it means, and I don't pretend I do. I can understand without a perfect understanding. He's shown me that. I can pop the cap and inhale deeply and fill myself with the gifts of gods who never were gods. Back in Old Lost Angels, before my deliverance to this deeper Cali-dirt expanse of lizards and diamondback seraphim, wildcat bishops and roadrunners, I shot sweet Afghan heroin into my rotting arms, between my toes and fingers, but I'm free now. *You think this isn't Paradise? You think this isn't Eden? Then you better think again, little Chloe. You better think again.* Drew is a Titan. You know a Titan by the thunder in his belly and the fire on his chapped lips.

We dine on rattlesnakes and hot green tea, and Drew Standish, he tells us the last days are here. We camp upon the threshold, just switch on the television, that ginormous 1975 Zenith in its composite-board, wood-grain cabinet, and astroglide the picture tubes. The thing gets no stations out here, no rabbit ears needed. We don't need networks and programming; we need only *noise*. We need only snow, electromagnetic noise, man, *semut bertengkar* as Indonesians say, which translates into something like "war of the ants." Radio waves, cosmic microwave background radiation. *Baby doll, dig this, okay? One percent of that crackly shit is light from the Big Bang, come down thirteen billion years to tickle your rods and cones.* Me, I didn't know shit about physics and cosmology before I left L.A. All I knew was the aching, all-devouring urgency of the next fix.

I'm barefoot up here as the day I was born, high on our hot tin roof, high on cultured spores and the words of Drew, but like Shadrach, Meshach, and Abednego in the fiery furnace of wicked King Nebuchadnezzar, like Indian fakirs gifted by Allah, like an Apollo heat shield, I firewalk without burns. I bathe in the all-forgiving, all-anointing, purifying eye of Old Man Ra, and I wait for the others to join me on the roof. I'm positively zealous, says Madeline, in my devotions and my sacrifices, the holy mortification of sloughing flesh, and she tells me the others could learn from my example. Sweaty rivulets scald my eyes, and I blink away the little pain. I keep my eyes on the Chocolate Mountains. *They'll come from there,* says Drew. *They will come from sunrise.*

I raise my arms in praise.

I just looked up one day, and he was looking down, and he offered me a hand.

And man, *that* was a goddamn first.

"It isn't your fault, little Chloe, that you fell so far. Chernobyl claims our souls. The opium kissed your blood to soothe the throb of NOW, and you fucked it and let it fuck you because no one else ever has loved you true and dear."

He held me while I cried. He held me in a filthy alley behind a filthy concrete squat somewhere in the void between Ninety-third and Ninety-fourth streets in Westmont. I smelled of shit and infection, sour sweat and Goodwill castoffs. In that spray-can graffiti gangland razor-wire palm-tree Inferno did he hold me tight (and, looking back, that was surely the treacherous Ninth Circle, me sunk and frozen to my throat in the ice of the River Cocytus). I had squandered teen ages behind me and my fast squandering twenties going down in rubble all around, but there he was, silver haired and beautiful, eyes like this sky above me today. He offered a hand and freedom and absolution, and all I had to do was crawl up from the Pit. From so far down, to so far up here, the mountains out before me and the Salton Sea evaporating at my back, dying its slow, slow inevitable inland death. I am poised between, being cooked same as H once bubbled molten in my junkie's spoon. I am being made ready for the coming evacuation of this ruined, forsaken planet.

"In those realms, the sun shines no brighter than a star," he tells us, Madeline and me and the others, as we watch the static and listen to the voices buried *in* the static, two waves superimposed to form the holy intersection of the Third Wave, mightier than the one plus the one, gathering half the deep and full of voices, we cling to him, and we slowly rise and wait to be plunged, roaring, and all the wave will be in a cold blue flame. And he says, "Behold the black rivers of pitch that flow under those mysterious cyclopean bridges."

I feel movement in my lungs, and I cough. I taste blood and mold at the back of my throat, and I spit on the roof. My spittle is thick and yellow; it sizzles.

I smile.

I smile a lot these days.

Drew scooped me up from that Dantean alleyway so that I'd remember how I smiled when I was just a kid and all my fears were only kid fears and all my horrors were only kid horrors. He wrapped me in a musty leather duster that I think he stole from a Clint Eastwood movie, and he put me in the front seat of that old red Buick station wagon he drives, and he ferried me back to life good as if Charon had changed his mind. Drew is a magician. He makes time run in all directions. Man, he makes time do his motherfucking bidding. They gave him that, power over clocks and wristwatches. And that day I listened as Madeline talked from the backseat and Drew followed the varicose labyrinth of numbered highway signs east and south, leaving the Big Orange in the back of us for the blessed sanctuary of a Sonoran promised land. Rolling me smooth on white-walled steel belts past enchanted places I'd never been—Palm Springs, Rancho Mirage, Indio, Thermal. When I saw the turnoff for Mecca, I asked, *Then this is it?* And he laughed that quicksilver laugh he laughs and shook his head. *No, little Chloe, but we're close now. Now we're very, very close.* Another few miles, and I got my first sight of the Salton Sea. I got my eyes full.

"I'll tell you stories," he said, "when you've got your bearings, stories about the how and the why and the when of it."

"You mean the water?"

"I mean it *all*, baby doll."

I lit a cigarette, breathed smoke and nicotine, and marveled at a great flat houseboat stranded at the side of the road like the skeleton of a dead whale. There was broken furniture scattered about on its deck, and the name written across its bow in letters faded not quite to illegibility was *Heart's Desire*.

"Last chance," Drew said, and I asked him, "Last chance for what?"

"Never mind," he said. "Never you mind, little Chloe. One day, I'll tell you what the Indians knew. One day real soon."

I stand in the sun. I stand on the broiling roof of the ranch house, and my feet have long since burned until they're callused and numb as if they were shot full of novocaine. I can hear the TV playing below me, its static choked up with voices, because in the mouth of the beast there are more beasts. I stand with my arms raised, feeling it all, hearing it all, thinking—just for an instant—maybe Drew got it wrong. Maybe my prophet is fallible, and in just a second or two more, I'm gonna come apart at the seams and scatter in a spray of photons and spores. Like, you know, those ancient crumbs of the Big Bang, spilling out across forever to reach an old TV set. I'll be the first of all those Little Bangs to come. I'll be both his Alpha and Omega, and he'll be proud and not for one second regret having found me and saved me from the needle's prick.

"Let me just ask you this," Drew says, whispering in my ear and speaking from some other day, from now and then and some tomorrow yet to come. He sounds like hellfire, sulfur, and silk sheets. "How much have you thought about what was really in back of that great digital switchover in 2013? The fact that it was *mandatory*, I mean. The forced cessation of analog transmissions, the goddamn Digital Television Transition and Public Safety Act of 2005? Congress, the FCC, the American Association of Broadcasters all talking about conserving electricity and how we're getting such better picture quality, right? Yeah, sure, but who is it pulls their strings? What's this really all about, because now not just anyone can switch on the tube and catch that sacred one-percent signal. In every cubic *centimeter* of the universe there are three hundred photons from the Big Bang. And SETI? That was just some hippie scientist boondoggle, and that's what's *really* going on here, see. You got these gatekeepers not wanting us to gaze into the oldest fossil in all Creation, the very face of God."

I hear the TV, and I can hear the others. Some of them are so much farther along than me. I'm not good about hiding my jealousy. I make no secret of the fact that I want to be the first to bloom, and that's okay, because humility ain't got no place in *their* plan.

"Stop and think, okay?" And Drew taps his finger hard against his forehead, the way he does when he's making a point. "Just stop and fucking think. The NTIA, OPAD, the Office of Spectrum Management, MediaFLO, fucking Microsoft, and definitely fucking Apple. You ever wondered about the Beatles and Apple? You ever looked at the label at the center of a *vinyl* copy of the Beatles' *Abbey Road* or *Let It Be*? Ever done all the correlative and concordance work linking all those Apple Records releases—Badfinger, Billy Preston, the Radha Krsna Temple, Doris goddamn Day and Ronnie Spector, Ravi Shankar, and et cetera and et cetera and et cetera—and seen where the siren trail leads, how it gets all tangled up in that Los Altos garage with Jobs, Wozniak, and Ronald Wayne? You ever thought about *why* Apple Inc. *is* Apple Inc.? That bullshit Jobs spun about his fruitarian diet, I seriously hope you're not gonna buy *that* crap. About Jobs' jobs in orchards and Sir Isaac Newton, the misdirection of that original logo with Newton sitting beneath a tree waiting to be struck by gravity? Yeah, they kinda showed their hand there, what with Yggdrasil, the Tree of Knowledge of Good and Evil, the Bodhi Tree, the Glastonbury Thorn—*Ficus religiosa* and *Crataegus monogyna,* respectively. 'A is for Apple,' yeah right, and I got a bridge you're gonna buy real cheap up in Cisco."

I want to open my eyes, the windows to my soul, but Drew reminds me it's too soon to burn out my retinas. I'm gonna need them just a little longer.

The station wagon, cherry red, rushed past the *Heart's Desire,* and Madeline was talking, then, about the tourist-trade, resort getaway boom and bust of the Salton Sea, about Sonny Bono and avian botulism. I listened, but her words were bleeding through me. My head was too full of sun and sea and earth.

"Did you know that between 1978 and 2006 Apple Records sued Apple Computer multiple times?" Drew asks his congregation. "That's another bit of misdirection. But the truth is that the music playing in that fateful Los Altos garage, Steve Jobs' parents' garage, it was *Let It Be, Abbey Road, Yellow Submarine,* and yeah, *The White Album.* But—wait, before you start in about that lunatic Manson—he got all that shit wrong. Manson was a cunt, and he was also crazier than a shithouse rat. No, you listen to 'Revolution 9,' okay?"

Rouge doctors have brought this specimen. 9, number 9, a man without terrors, only to find the night-watchman, unaware of his presence in the building.

Below me, I hear the screen door bang shut, so here they come, the others, and in a moment they climb up the ladder, and I won't be alone with the heat, with the Chocolate Mountains and the jackrabbits. I won't be alone with Drew's precious whispers. Some days, I'd like to murder the lot of them, if only that were part of the plan. By now, they're probably partway to the rickety ladder leading up to the roof and me.

Take this brother, it may serve you well. Eldorado, if you become naked.

I turn my back on the mountains and face the white and stinking Salton Sea.

3.

Zero-Sum Gethsemane
(July 10, 2015)

BACK AT LA POSADA, the Signalman sits on the edge of his bed in a sweat-stained T-shirt and his Fruit of the Loom briefs, waiting on morning. It's not quite half past two. He pours himself another shot of J&B, filling the paper Dixie cup almost precisely one third of the way. He's taking it slow, pacing himself. The bottle needs to last until dawn. Right now, the thought of running out of whisky before he runs out of night is sufficient incentive to marshal the iron fist of self-control. That might change a little later on. It's still early, after all, and the demons dancing about behind his eyes are the very competitive sort. The contents of Immacolata Sexton's fancy briefcase versus sobriety. The fear of his dreams versus exhaustion. You get the picture. The AC purrs like a cat made of ice. The curtains are pulled shut, and the television's on. Clark Gable is helping Claudette Colbert make her way up the Eastern Seaboard, from Florida to New York City. True love is on the line, or so she thinks. Albany's best man sips his J&B and stares at the screen for a while, before turning his attention back to the thick dossier the Y operative handed over at the diner. He's pacing himself with that, too.

The life and times and crimes of Mr. Drew Standish.

All that's known, plus some guesswork, plus just a little bit more.

The Signalman lights another cigarette. At fifty-five, he remembers when it wasn't necessary to disable the smoke alarms of hotel rooms. Too often, it occurs to him that he's lived just long enough to have completely out-lived the world that made sense to him, the world where he fit. He's as good as a goddamn dinosaur.

He picks up a sheaf of typed pages held together with a green plastic paper clip. It's obvious they were typed, that it isn't a printout, since almost all the *o*'s and 8s are punched through. The page on top, a coffee-stained memorandum from Barbican Estate to its offices in Dubai, is dated October 12, 1999. Standish was a busy little beaver that year, that long string of red-letter days for doomsayers and cultists of every stripe. Never mind that the whole Y2K thing was a washout, a false alarm, a tempest in a teapot of hype. There'd be plenty of second chances for Standish, all of them leading—in hind-sight—straight to that sun-blasted shack in the Coachella Valley.

The Signalman flips through the report, only bothering to scan every other paragraph, then drops it onto the bed with the rest. It's hard to concentrate. Faced with all this shit and alone with only his thoughts, half a pint of 70-proof Scotch, and old movies for company, he keeps flashing back to the ranch. That was eight days ago now, but it hardly seems like eight hours. Time's moving too fast for him to keep up, and even with London's prompt cooperation and the package that ghoul dressed up like a woman delivered, he feels like he's chasing his own tail. Whatever revelations and helpful, relevant patterns might eventually be gleaned from the dossier, that's work for someone else, someone with distance and clarity. Someone who wasn't on the ground during the raid on Standish's compound.

He takes another dry swallow of whisky, trying to forget the sickly, musty taste of the air trapped inside that house. No such luck, not tonight, probably not ever. He rubs his eyes, then stares at the television screen. Clark Gable is munching a carrot and lecturing the runaway Ellen Andrews. He looks like Bugs Bunny. Sounds a little like him, for that matter. *You can't be scared and hungry at the same time,* he says. *If you're scared, it scares the hunger out of you.* Sure, that Peter Warne, he's one smart cookie. Before it's over, he'll get the scoop *and* the dame.

Out on Route 66, a driver leans hard on their horn,

the sound stretched and distorted by the Doppler shift. In his room, the Signalman jumps, startled, immediately embarrassed and wondering why the fuck anyone would blow their horn on an empty highway at two thirty in the goddamn morning. But maybe there was an animal crossing the road. Maybe it was a coyote or an armadillo or Good ol' Señor Chupacabra, come round to pay its respects.

He takes a drag on his cigarette and glances at the empty briefcase lying open on the bed, yawning like the jaws of a stylish, toothless carnivore.

I can't forget it. I'm still hungry, says Ellen Andrews, speaking from the celluloid ghost of 1934. And then the Signalman's restless mind slips back to Friday again, that moment when he draws his revolver and steps through the doorway, crossing the threshold, and, sure, he knows better because he's already relived, replayed, revisited it all a hundred times by now, but he does it anyway.

The house is full of sunlight and shadows.

And the smell of toadstools.

He's right behind Vance, close enough he can see the beads of perspiration standing out on her brow and upper lip, and he's wondering why she's on point. Coming up the drive, wasn't she two cars behind him? Crossing that maze of drooping cacti and rusted automobiles, wasn't he in the lead?

There's nothing much in the front room but broken furniture and even more dust and sand, he thinks, than there is outside. He follows Vance into the kitchen and spots a dead scorpion in the sink, belly up atop a stack of filthy dishes. Off the kitchen, there's a narrow hallway, and now he can hear television static coming from one of the bedrooms. The mushroomy stink is worse back here. A lot worse.

"Place is empty," says someone behind him, Malinowski or one of the FBI mooks who haven't yet figured out they're in way over their pay grade and over their heads. "We missed him. Shitbird's probably halfway to fucking Tijuana by now."

There's a calendar on the wall by the fridge, the sort you get free at Chinese restaurants. Someone's circled July third. He looks up to find that Vance is already in the hallway, and the Signalman hesitates, starts to call her back, opens his mouth, then shuts it again. He winces at a sudden burst of white noise from the radio Velcroed to his bulletproof vest. That hall, it makes him think of a slaughterhouse chute. No room to turn around in there. No room to fucking fight.

You getting the heebie-jeebies, old man? Aren't you the one who never flinched?

"Wait," he says, but his voice seems very small in the heat and the reek, small and entirely devoid of authority.

"Hold up, Vance, I want to get eyes on—"

Cool as shit through a polar bear, wasn't that you?

And then he sees the look on her face, and even without seeing whatever she sees, he knows it's bad. "Oh my god," she whispers. "Oh god. Fuck me . . ."

The Signalman picks up the remote and turns off the TV. He stubs out his cigarette and goes to the bathroom. His urine is dark, concentrated, the color of apple juice. He wonders how long until he winds up with kidney stones. His old man had them. Howled in pain like a dying hound dog, and isn't *that* something to look forward to? He washes his hands with a tiny bar of Ivory soap, then pauses to stare at himself in the mirror. The fluorescent lights make his skin seem thin as vellum, and he rubs his fingers over the salt-and-pepper stubble on his cheeks and chin. He should shave. He won't feel like it in the morning, hungover and late for his train. If he shaves now, it's an excuse not to go back to the dossier on Drew Standish and all the nightmares contained therein, all the warning signs nobody heeded until, as they say, it was too late.

If he concentrates on shaving, maybe he can stave off the memory of what they found at the end of that hallway and, a little later, huddled on the roof. The sight of those bodies, and the smell.

It's actually a number of species of fungus existing together in a symbiotic mass, Ophiocordyceps unilateralis, *often referred to by a more colorful and more pronounceable moniker, zombie fungus. It attacks a particular family of tropical ants, known as camponitids, or carpenter ants, entering the hosts' bodies during the yeast stage of its complex reproductive cycle. The fungus spreads through an ant's body, maturing inside its head—and this is where things really get interesting. It eventually takes control of the infected insect, forcing it to latch on to the underside of a leaf and bite down in what we call the grip of death. Then atrophy sets in, quickly, completely destroying the sarcomere connections in the ant's muscle fibers and reducing its sarcoplasmic reticula and mitochondria. At this point, the ant is no longer able to control the muscles of the mandible and will remain fixed in place. The fungus finally kills the ant and continues to grow as hyphae penetrate the soft tissues and begin to structurally fortify the ant's exoskeleton. Mycelia sprout and securely anchor it to the leaf, at the same time secreting antimicrobial compounds that ward off competition from other* Ophiocordyceps *colonies.*

In the mirror, his eyes seem more gray than blue, and the broken capillaries in his nose are as good as a road map, tracing decades and countless drinking binges. But he's a prime asset, and as long as he gets the job done, Albany is happy to overlook the booze. With luck, they'll squeeze another ten years out of him. He turns on the tap and splashes warm water across his face, then reaches for the can of shaving cream he left on the back of the toilet.

And get this, okay? These doomed ants, these poor dying bastards, they always climb to a height of precisely twenty-five point twenty plus or minus two point forty-six centimeters above the jungle floor, in environments where the humidity will remain stable between ninety-four and ninety-five percent, with temperatures between twenty and thirty Celsius. And always on the north side of the plant. In the end, sporocarps, the fungal fruiting bodies, erupt from the ant's necking, growing a stalk that releases spores that'll infect more ants. It's evolution at its best and, yeah, at its most grisly, too. Mother Nature, when you get right down to it, she's a proper cunt.

But these weren't ants. These were human beings.

Well, sure, and this isn't Ophiocordyceps, *either. We're not even sure if it's an actual fungus. No one's ever seen anything like it. Jesus, if I didn't know better, I'd say it came from outer space.*

If you didn't know better.

Right.

The mirror is starting to fog from the steam, and *there's* a small bit of mercy. The Signalman squirts a mound of foam into his left hand, but can't quite find the motivation to go any further. Who gives a shit if he's clean shaven when he gets back to L.A.? Maybe he'll tell them he's decided to grow a beard. At least it would hide some of the damage wrought by time and his bad habits, wouldn't it? And isn't that what Albany's all about? Hiding the damage? He rinses the foam off his hand and turns off the water.

That day they all found Hell by the Salton Sea, that day that's still unfurling inside his mind, Agent Vance is bracing herself against a doorframe. She's lowered her gun and covers her mouth, trying not to vomit. "Oh god," she says again, the words muffled, and she looks at him. Right then, he thinks, *I've never seen anyone so scared.* It's not true, not by a long shot, but that's what he thinks, all the same.

I know an old lady who swallowed a fly. . . .

What?

I don't know. It's been stuck in my head all damned day long.

Past the corpses, what's left of three girls and two boys, none of them older than sixteen or seventeen, there's an old television set, a real antique, just like his parents bought when he was a kid. The first color TV they ever owned. There's nothing on the screen but static, a blizzard of white electric snow. It crawls across the curved screen like ants. It drifts behind the glass like deadly spores carried on the wind.

"Stop the choppers," he says into the radio, even

though he's not yet entirely sure *why* he's giving the order. Some instinct buried deep in his hindbrain, spurring him to act before higher cognition gets in the way of survival. "Get Edwards on the line and set up a no-fly zone, everything from Palm Springs south to Mexicali. Get roadblocks up."

The radio crackles and spurts, and the man on the other end wants to know why.

"Because I fucking just said so," he growls. "Because I imagine you want to keep your fucking job."

He hears footsteps on the tin roof.

Alfred Russel Wallace, he was the first to identify the fungus, in Brazil way back in 1859. Yeah, Wallace. You know, the dude who almost beat Darwin to the punch? Don't you people read?

In his room by the railroad tracks, the Signalman dries his face on a towel embroidered with the hotel's logo. He spares one last glance at his haggard reflection, and then goes back to the bed, back to the files and the briefcase and his whisky, back to waiting for the long Arizona night to end.

4.

A Piece of the Sky
(August 17, 1968)

AND NOW, PICK UP this silver, open-face watch, which the Signalman carries always tucked into the narrow left inside breast pocket of the cheap suits he wears. It was the property of one of his four great-grandfathers before him, and he's carried it since the day she died. It is this watch that will earn him his nickname. His mother kept it in an old Whitman's sampler tin on her dresser. Pick up this tarnished silver watch, manufactured in 1888 by the Elgin Watch Company of Elgin, Illinois, and wind the stem counterclockwise, turning the hands back 34,256 full revolutions. By this action do we arrive at the evening of August 17, 1968, and the living room of a house on the outskirts of Birmingham, Alabama. It's Saturday night, and NBC affiliate WVTM, Channel 13, is airing its weekly late-night triple-feature monster-movie marathon. The child who will someday be known to his coworkers, and a few others, as "the Signalman" is eight years old, and he's allowed to stay up Friday nights (into Saturday mornings) to watch these black-and-white gems. While his parents sleep, the boy is treated to Ray Harryhausen's Rhedosaurus, Charles Laughton's Quasimodo, and, finally, English director James Whale's little-known and once-believed-lost *The Star Maiden* (1934).

As with his classic *Frankenstein,* Whale chose the palette of Gothic horror for this science-fiction/fantasy tale set on an undiscovered trans-Neptunian tenth planet located beyond newly discovered Pluto, "near the farthest edges of the solar system." The special effects come courtesy Willis O'Brien, fresh off *King Kong* and *Son of Kong,* with an unnerving, distinctly modernist score provided by Max Steiner (another *Kong* vet), and a screenplay by none other than Tarzan-creator Edgar Rice Burroughs. *The Star Maiden* marks the only time that Burroughs would write for the screen.

The boy sips at a Coca-Cola, the soda gone flat from half a handful of salted peanuts he dropped into the bottle, and he tries hard to stay awake. But it's a rare Friday night that he manages to make it through all three features. He's drifting off, and the movie is beginning to blur together with half-formed dreams. Tomorrow, he'll have trouble remembering which bits of the story were actually part of the movie and which bits he made up in his sleep:

A willowy woman with white hair is locked in a black tower in a city at the edge of a blacker plain. From her prison, she gazes out through barred windows, across the weird angles of a city carved from obsidian and onyx, granite and slate, across rooftops and strange hanging gardens and past the spires of other towers. Overhead, the sun is only a faint smudge peering down at this world through a veil of perpetual night. The white-haired woman has been shut away by an evil, ancient man, who might be an alchemist, or a scientist, or a wizard (this is never made quite clear) and who intends the woman to be his bride, very much against her will. Her only hope for deliverance is a sword that can defeat the dragonlike, stop-motion beast that guards the tower gates. But the sword was lost long ages ago in a dimly remembered war between the people of this world and giants who attempted to invade and conquer it from another dimension. There is a hero, of course, a handsome man with hair as pale as the woman's. He eludes the alchemist's robot soldiers and travels far from the city to reclaim the sword, which, it turns out, was stolen by a grotesque race of winged, crablike humanoids, creatures who inhabit a forest of immense glowing fungi—tall as redwoods—at the edge of an underground sea. They worship the very beings who were once defeated by the magical sword, hiding it in hopes that someday those extradimensional titans will return.

The creatures speak in a language that sounds like the buzzing of bees.

Back at the black tower, the villain wields an enormous spyglass and confides in his prisoner, revealing to her the recent discovery of a planet orbiting much nearer to the sun, a paradise of blues and greens, which he intends to conquer and enslave with a deadly heat ray. Then, he tells her, they will travel together through the aether to rule over this new domain as its rightful king and queen. Just how this trip will be accomplished is never fully explained, but the method of conveyance is clearly nothing so mundane as a rocket ship.

"Only our minds," says the alchemist, "need leave this sphere and make the long, cold journey through the dark. These bodies we wear are no more, my love, than tattered garments we've outgrown. In the new world we'll have *new* forms, *new* bodies."

Two surgeons are summoned, stooped men who look more like vultures, and the white-haired woman is sedated with a drop of some narcotic tincture. The surgeons then strap a bizarre metal cap over her head, preparing to cut open the skull and remove the brain. Meanwhile, our hero, who has managed against all odds to wrest the sword from the claws of the flying crustaceans, battles the dragon thing that guards the tower gates.

The maiden. The mad scientist. The champion.

Three crisply drawn archetypes.

Think of them as tarot cards.

Think of the film as a reading.

According to the *Los Angeles Times* and various other newspapers and tabloids, the actress who played the heroine in *The Star Maiden* died a mere five weeks after production wrapped, having sustained massive brain injuries in an automobile accident. The irony hasn't been lost on the morbid sort of movie buff who catalogs so-called cursed films. While the fact of her death is well documented, there are rumors that she'd become paranoid and left behind a diary with a very peculiar final entry, several pages that rambled on about nightly visits by "tall men in black suits" who came to the windows and watched her when they thought she was sleeping. They spoke in "buzzes and clicks," she's supposed to have written.

The actor who played the alchemist, he died the next year of a morphine overdose, after his homosexual love affair with a much younger screenwriter became common knowledge among his peers. He appears to have had connections to a number of hermetical and theosophical societies and to have corresponded during the last three years of his life with Aleister Crowley and other occultists.

As for the hero of the tale, he left acting in 1936 and moved to New Mexico, where he wrote a pair of science-fiction novels, *Starlost* and *Sunfall,* neither of which was ever published and both of which amounted to little more than barely coherent theories about life on Venus and Mars, a secret Martian base beneath the desert, and the role he believed aliens to have had in the emergence of Communism and the October Revolution. He was found dead in 1946, long after *The Star Maiden* was all but forgotten, the last print believed to have been destroyed in a Burbank theater fire.

And there was the cameraman who is said to have hanged himself during filming.

And the makeup artist who might have died a few hours after the premiere.

And the strangers said by some, including the director, to have haunted the set, men in dark suits who come off sounding an awful lot like the actress's Peeping Toms.

Make of this what you will or make of it nothing at all.

Ten minutes from THE END, the eight-year-old boy loses his struggle, slipping from half awake to fast asleep. It'll be twenty-six years and then some before he learns how it all played out, whether the maiden was rescued and the villain defeated. Twenty-six years before he's known to those few who know him as "the Signalman" and he's shown how the film thinly disguised as fiction a nightmare that unfolded on a remote Vermont farm in 1927. How it foreshadowed still other more ominous events in the decades after its release. One day, it will lead him, however indirectly, to a run-down diner in Winslow, Arizona.

The best foreshadowing never *seems* like foreshadowing.

5.

Last of the Hobo Kings (Shining Road) (July 10, 2015)

BENEATH A SKY OF brutal blue, Engine 69 drags its silver snake, rattling and swaying and clanking along the Atchison, Topeka and Santa Fe. It pulled out of Flagstaff fifteen minutes ago, rolling west across the Colorado Plateau. In his sleeper car, the Signalman sits with his back turned to the engine, looking east, the way they've come. He doesn't like that vacant shade of blue hanging above the afternoon, and so he keeps his eyes on the green-brown patchwork of scrub and ponderosa pine. Snowcapped Mount Elden is growing small in the train's wake and the Flagstaff skyline has been entirely lost to view. Only a hazy veil of smog remains to mark its place. Immacolata's briefcase sits at his feet. Thanks to the fresh bottle of Scotch he picked up before boarding the *Southwest Chief,* he already has enough of a buzz that the night before is beginning to lose its edge. He's thinking maybe he'll even catch a little shut-eye before L.A., now that he's finished writing out his report. Sure thing. A few more shots, and sleep won't be so hard at all.

But then there's a knock at the door to his compartment, four sharp raps, and at first he figures it's just one of the attendants, because who the hell else would it be. An attendant, or maybe another passenger who's mistaken the Signalman's sleeper for their own. But when he draws back the blue privacy curtain, the face of the man standing in the corridor is all too fucking familiar. And right now, maybe it's not the very last face he wants to see, but it's certainly high on the list. He briefly allows himself to entertain the fantasy that he won't open the door, that he'll pretend not to recognize the ferrety eyes and crooked nose, the thin lips and jutting chin. *You got the wrong man, bub. So just keep moving. Louse up some other poor slob's day.*

It's nice while it lasts, all four or five seconds, and then he pops the latch, tugs at the handle, and slides the door open. The noise from the corridor pours in, washing over and through him, like the rumbling, discordant notes of the bullbitch hangover he's got coming. The man—whose name is Jack Dunaway—nods once, smiles, and there's a glimmer in his small, dark eyes as he steps into the compartment. The Signalman fakes a smile in return, then shuts the door behind him and locks it again.

Jack Dunaway takes a seat. He's fifteen years younger

than the Signalman, and he looks it. He was recruited out of MIT, towards the end of George W's administration.

"Got on in Flagstaff," he says.

"Well, I didn't imagine you parachuted onto the roof like Roger fucking Moore," replies the Signalman, and he follows the man's gaze to the briefcase.

"That's it?" asks Dunaway.

"Yeah, that's it. You think I'd be headed back empty-handed?"

"Fuck, you never know, right? Tell me, was she as bad as people say?"

"Bad? I think I'd want to have a few more colorful adjectives at my disposal before I tried my hand at describing her. What the fuck are you doing here, Jack? What is it couldn't wait a few more hours until I'm back in Los Angeles?"

The man glances out the window. "A shame they stuck you on this side of the train. From the other side, you can see the San Francisco Peaks. It's what's left of a prehistoric volcano. Did you know that?"

"I've had enough scenery to last me awhile," he says, and takes a sip of whisky, making a point of not offering Dunaway a drink. "You didn't answer my question."

Jack's eyes dart from the southern view to the Signalman, then back to the window and the desert rushing past on the other side of the tinted glass.

"I'm afraid you're not going back to L.A. You're getting off at Williams Junction. We have you flying out of Clark at six seventeen this evening."

The Signalman wants to punch Dunaway in the face.

"I don't fly," he says.

"They need you at Groom Lake."

"Fuck Groom Lake. I don't fucking fly, you know I don't fucking fly, and besides, Dispatch said I could stand down after running courier to Winslow. Send Vance."

"We're sending you," says Jack Dunaway. He doesn't sound annoyed or impatient; he just sounds bored.

"Fuck that. Send Vance."

"Well, that would have been my first choice, but Vance is benched for the duration. Maybe longer."

"What the hell for?"

"You got a lot of anger in you, you know that? A guy your age, that's not so good for the ticker. All that anger and all the hooch."

"Groom Lake is Vance's neck of the woods," says the Signalman, letting the observation about his temperament slide. It's not like it isn't true.

Dunaway glances at the bottle of J&B, then takes one of the disposable plastic cups from the sink and helps himself. He squints at the sunlight through the window.

"She came up red last night. She's already in quarantine in Atlanta. Anyway, Albany doesn't want Vance, they want you, and you'll be on that plane."

But the Signalman doesn't hear that last part. He doesn't make it past *She came up red last night.* Suddenly there's an icy knot in his bowels that no amount of whisky's ever gonna burn away. He stares at Dunaway, and Dunaway stares back at him.

"How's that even possible? She went through decon. We were all clean."

Dunaway shakes his head, sort of shrugs, almost smiles. "Man, you take the cake, you know that? After all these years, you're still out here bothering with *why* and *how.* I don't fucking know how it happened. She came up positive. That's what they told me, so that's what I know. How about you stop busting my balls?" He screws the cap back on the bottle and offers it to the Signalman.

You smug little shit, he thinks. *When's the last time you so much as got your hands dirty?* The Signalman empties his cup, then refills it halfway. He sets the bottle on the floor by the briefcase, safely out of Dunaway's reach.

"Anyone else?" he asks.

"Anyone else what?" Dunaway wants to know.

"Is Vance the only positive so far?"

"From the team, yeah. As far as I know. That's all they've told me."

"So nothing from California? No bad news from Bombay Beach?"

"Dude, if you'd bother to check in more often, you might be a little more up on current events. As far as I know, no cases in the hot zone. Of course, we both know that means next to zilch, what with the epidemiologists still stuck trying to suss out exactly what we're dealing with."

"We know what we're dealing with," says the Signalman, wanting a cigarette so badly, his hands are shaking.

Dunaway does that almost-laughing thing again. "Right, well, you're just going to have to excuse me for not drinking Standish's purple Kool-Aid. If you want to, go right on ahead, but I'm waiting for something a little more scientific than a madman's gibberish about extraterrestrial mildew from Planet X."

The Signalman takes out his half-empty pack of Camels, opens it, then puts it away again. Look at the bright side, right? With Williams Junction coming up fast, at least he can grab a goddamn smoke or five before they shove him onto the plane to Nevada.

"You're just made out of bad habits, aren't you?" smirks Dunaway.

The Signalman ignores him. "You weren't there. You didn't see it." And he wants to start ticking off the long, long list of shit this thirtysomething asshole hasn't seen and doesn't know and apparently can't imagine, but what's the point. Here's the next generation sitting across from him, the future of the Company just waiting around for the gullible old Cold War spooks like him to retire. The future so bright and all that happy crap. One good thing he can say for Barbican Estate, you don't hear all this skeptical, rationalist mumbo jumbo from the agents of Y.

"Whatever you say. I'm just here to make sure you don't find some way to fuck up and miss that flight. You want to believe in little green men, you go right ahead. Toss in the Easter Bunny, I won't argue."

"What about the case?" the Signalman asks Dunaway.

"It goes with you. I'll take your report, you keep the case."

The Signalman nods. "We didn't used to be so damned sloppy," he says. He's thinking about Vance reading clean, then reading hot. And he's also thinking about all the people he's had contact with since he was released from quarantine: L.A., Winslow, the train and taxis, restaurants and bars, the hotel. What does that come to? Five hundred, maybe? More than? And all *those* people, how many have they had contact with? If he's infected, how many thousands of opportunities has the contagion enjoyed at his expense? He shuts his eyes and concentrates on the rhythm of the steel wheels against the rails.

The end of the world as exponential growth.

"I don't need a fucking babysitter," he says.

"And I don't need a gig as your keeper, but there you go."

The Signalman doesn't say anything else. He just keeps his eyes shut, trying not to think about Vance locked away somewhere and dying. Yeah, man, good luck with that.

6.

The Beginning After the End
(July 2, 2015)

"YOU ARE SO BEAUTIFUL," Drew tells us, me and Madeline and all the faceless others. They have, to me, become faceless. "All of you, each one, so perfect. You are my dreams made manifest. We are the children of all the eons. You are the path unto deliverance. There are no accidents here." I'd say that the television sounds like a waterfall, except I've never been to a waterfall, only heard them recorded, and recordings are only echoes, and echoes can lie. So, I'll say that the television sounds like rain on the streets of a fallen city I'll never have to see again. Not ever, and that's a promise. We sit within the mandala Drew has scratched into the floor of the room with the television. My God, this room is filled with ghosts, and those are echoes, too. I can hear them, and I can see them. I don't know if the others can. Last night, when I told Drew, when I only whispered about the ghosts because maybe they can hear *me*, he said it was a sign of the nearness of the star winds. That gave

me chill bumps, sent something small and frightened scurrying across the grave that I will never have. And now, we sit here in the night with the television blaring white-static wasp voices and the night wrapped tight about the house like a wet towel. Drew reads to us from the Black Book. He has told Madeline (she has told me) that he found the book in Iran, where it had been hidden since the Achaemenid Empire, a.k.a. the First Persian Empire, in the year 352 B.C., when it was placed in the tomb of—well, he never reads the name aloud. Some things are like that, he assures us. You do not say some words out loud. You only know them, and you only dare mutter them in dreams.

The Black Book revealed us all to Drew. Our names are written there.

We are not permitted to see the pages of the book.

I don't mind.

"This is how long we have waited," he says. "So many ragged centuries have the promises lain unfulfilled, gathering the weight of seconds and minutes and hours, while the messengers from Yuggoth prepared the way, while they mined what they needed from this world to build eternal cities for our souls."

He turns a page.

The girl he found in Seattle tries to speak, and he pauses in his reading to listen. The noises she makes are no longer precisely words. We all think that she will be

the first. She was pretty once, and now, transformed, she is beautiful. No, that's still too small a word. "A flower," Madeline says. "She will fold open like a rose, and the star winds will come pouring down from the sky and down from the mountains to scour the rocks and lift her up to the heavens. As you each shall be lifted." We have to carry her up to and down from the roof now, the girl from Seattle. In the gray light from the television, her skin shimmers with colors I don't know the names for. She was afraid, a few days ago, but now I don't think she is. Fear of the passage is an affront to the messengers, Drew says. Fear is a poison that binds the minds of men and women to the same stone where Prometheus' liver is devoured forever by the cruel beaks of hungry birds.

Yesterday, I forgot my name. It was an odd sensation, realizing I no longer knew what my mother and father had christened me, a few seconds of cold panic. But the panic was fleeting, and behind it was peace and assurance. We can't carry our names with us on the journey that lies ahead.

Drew sets the metal cylinder at the center of the mandala. That will be his chariot across the void. Madeline also has a silvery tube. When we are complete, those of us whom he has brought here to the garden, then he and Madeline will have their own passage, which is not to be the same as ours.

I believe my thoughts do not flow as they once did.

I can almost remember being some other way.

He reads from the book the lines about the flood, and the lines about the crack in the earth that lies below the waters of the flood. The book calls the flood Jachin, and it calls the crack Boaz. We were all taught the wrong words for things, a sleight of hand perpetrated by the Old Ones who would forever delay our escape. We were taught to call the crack San Andreas, and we were taught to call the flood Salton. In names is all the power of a splitting atom, and if you steal names, you steal hope. I go down to sleep each night, and swim among the fish that swim the flood. The tilapia are iridescent angels that glide silently above the muddy, silt-shrouded bottom, and the sun filters down through the seraphim phantoms of croakers and orangemouth corvina. "On a day very soon," says Drew, "Boaz will shudder, and Jachin will murder her own. And we'll know, then, that the day has arrived.

"It's so close now. Cross my heart and hope to die. Bo and Peep, Doe and Ti, as you are the Children of the Next Level."

There isn't only the television and the burring voices buried in the static. There's also an old record playing on the turntable, a diamond needle setting free the Beatles even as our blooming shells will soon set free our souls and even as the fruit of our passage will liberate a million more. The music is a counterpoint to the TV, and it gives me comfort. So, we have the commingled symphony of white noise, the messengers, Lennon and McCartney, and the words read from the Black Book. Taken together, this is the Third of Seven Trumpets. *And the name of the star is called Wormwood: and the third part of the waters became wormwood; and many men died of the waters, because they were made bitter.* It's a poem, we are told, and a poem is a metaphor, and we take the stanzas literally at our own peril.

Just before dawn, I watched the lights that sometimes come to wake us, blue and crimson and purple. The lights that dance above the desert and dance above the house and dance above us all.

"Did you hear that?"

"Did I hear what?" I asked the boy that Drew and Madeline found in a whorehouse in Las Vegas.

"It was like someone crying, a long ways off."

"No, I didn't hear that," I answered, and then I asked him not to talk so much.

When was that?

My memories are like the waters that flow down to Jachin, losing themselves to the brine, saltier than the sea.

Drew closes the book and lays it next to the cylinder. Beyond the thin walls of the house, the messengers are moving about, and they are as angels. Their wings tremble at a frequency that sets our bones to humming. They click their chitinous song, so here's another layer added to the symphony. *Blackbird singing in the dead of night, all your life, you were only waiting, take these broken arms, my broken heart, our ruined lives, and fold us into thee. Blackbird singing . . .*

Seven for a secret never to be told.

All will be revealed.

The girl from Seattle sort of whimpers, and "Hush," Drew says. "Hush, hush, hushabye, my sweet."

Blackbird singing . . .

I bow my head (which isn't as easy as it was yesterday), and I listen to Drew as he translates for us.

"It begins here, with the seeds of your becoming, but the star winds will be a ferry, bearing the gift of the messengers far and wide. All those devils in their secret bunkers and Federal marble halls, all their conspiracies and machineries will have been for nothing. Their plots will be undone by each inhalation of the very same ones they've tried to damn. You will be drawn in through unsuspecting mouths and nostrils, down throats into lungs and bellies. So fuck their digital revolution, and fuck their Office of Spectrum Management. In the end, it will profit them not one whit. The faceless agents in their black suits and narrow ties, those sons of bitches who did their best to bury the Holy Visitations at Kecksburg, Roswell, Tunguska, Spitsbergen island, Paradise Valley. Call them X, Y, Z. Call them what the fuck ever. They've lied, and they've intimidated all the world over. They show up on doorsteps. They peer through windows, keyholes, and glory holes. They intimidate and spew false intimations. They are the demigods of stasis, and this is the week of their downfall, come round at last."

I want to close my eyes now.

Soon, pilgrim. Soon.

Thud. Skitter. Thump. The messengers are on the roof now.

"They came to a fortunate, chosen man in Vermont, way back in the autumn of the year 1927. But those faceless men interceded, and sure, they might have won *that* round, but what's on its way, they'll rue the day. When the globe becomes a grove, and the sky is sooty with clouds born of the believers' cast-off shells, they'll weep at the futility of all their sour endeavors. Even now, children, they scheme and scramble, deluded, drawing plans for that final battle. All in vain. They'll roll through the night in black panel vans and ebony Cadillacs, four horses of a misbegotten apocalypse. They'll come to our door. But they'll come too late."

Hosanna.

World without end.

Amen.

7

All Along the Watchtower/Midnight City
(1927, 1979, 2015, 2043, & etc.)

YOU ARE WHO YOU ARE, until you aren't anymore.

This is the First Law.

Thirty-nine thousand feet above the North Atlantic, Immacolata Sexton surfs the oily waves and troughs of Then, and Now, and What Will Be. The steel thrum of the Gulfstream G280's turbofan engines are the best lullaby she has ever known, and she's just about heard them all. Though her eyes may well be open, and though she may respond when the flight attendant speaks to her, her present cognitive state in no way resembles wakefulness. The plane races towards England at Mach 0.80, while the consciousness imprisoned in her living corpse knows no meaningful speed limits and travels in all directions simultaneously. She is the perfect voyager day-tripping an ever-expanding continuum of space and time without ever leaving her seat. She's a quantum-foam tourist, unanchored, unfettered, and her hajj has neither a beginning nor an end. Number lines are for squares.

She blinks, and it's a freezing February morning two days after the Ayatollah Ruhollah Mūsavi Khomeini ousted the Shah and seized control of Iran. Six days ago, Pluto moved inside the orbit of Neptune. Eleven days ago, Sid Vicious died of a heroin overdose. Immacolata Sexton dog-ears the hour. Tomorrow, the American ambassador to Afghanistan will be kidnapped by Muslim extremists. She bookmarks the minutes and sets out signposts at each and every millisecond. It wouldn't do to get lost in here.

The sky is the color of lead.

She's walking slowly across the frozen Scituate Reservoir, a few miles west of Providence, Rhode Island. An inch or so of fresh snow crunches beneath her boots, and the sheriff's deputy has mentioned twice now that she isn't dressed for the weather. Not far from the Route 14 Causeway, there's a hole punched through the ice. Cracks extend out from it like the radial strands of a spiderweb. The wind across the reservoir sounds lost.

"Where is the man who saw it?" she asks. The deputy stares at her a moment before answering, "We sent him home, but it's not far from here," he tells her.

He looks frightened.

"I'll need to speak with him," she says.

"Of course, ma'am. That shouldn't be a problem."

He thinks that she's NSA, and that story should hold just long enough for her to see what she needs to see. A little farther south, a clever bit of misdirection from London has the two agents from Albany chasing their tails round and round the mulberry bush. By the time they shake it off and get their bearings, she'll be long gone. It's a violation of three different interagency accords, but these things happen. With luck, everyone will be grown-ups about it.

"He figured maybe it was a satellite," says the deputy.

"Is that what he told you?"

"Yes, ma'am. He said it sorta slowed down and leveled off just before it hit the ice, like maybe it was aiming to make it to those trees over there," and the deputy points a gloved finger towards the line of oaks and maples on the eastern bank. "But I told him that didn't make a lot of sense. Not like a satellite's gonna have a pilot inside or anything, right? He also wondered if maybe it might be some sort of airplane, but that hole's just too small. For an airplane, I mean."

The hole is roughly teardrop shaped, slightly more that twelve feet across at its widest point, with the narrow end oriented towards the north, the direction from which the witness said the thing that fell from the sky came.

He said that it fell burning.

He said that it screamed.

There are odd marks on the ice, partly obscured by the light snow that's still falling, marks that suggest the object may have skidded a hundred yards or so before breaking through and sinking to the muddy bottom of the reservoir fifty feet below.

The deputy says, "The man we talked with at Brown, the astronomer, he thinks it was most likely nothing but a meteorite."

"Most likely," she says.

The object was picked up by air traffic controllers at Logan and T. F. Green and was briefly tracked from Hanscom Air Force Base in Bedford, Massachusetts. The latter estimated it was moving at about two thousand miles an hour, several times slower than any meteor's descent. The fireball was seen all across New England and Upstate New York.

The wind rearranges Immacolata's black hair and ruffles her blouse. She checks her wristwatch, then glances at the gray sky. She pulls up the collar of her coat, just for show.

"But I'm figuring," the deputy says, "no way the government's gonna bother sending someone out just for a falling star. More like, and I'm just guessing here, mind you, it's something the Soviets or the Red Chinese put up there. Something the Commies made for spying on us."

"You mean a reconnaissance satellite," she says, then

glances at him, her expression neither encouraging nor discouraging his speculation. He's talking so much because he's scared, and better he talk than stare at her and start asking himself *those* questions. "You read a lot, Officer?" she asks.

"Not especially," he replies. "Who's got the time, right? But I got a pretty good idea what the Commies are up to overhead. I mean, Reagan's always warning us. And I just figure that's why you're here. Otherwise, well, it would be someone like that professor at Brown. Or no one at all. Not if it was just a rock. You think maybe it's radioactive?"

She doesn't answer him. Instead, she squats down and brushes away the snow, then presses a naked palm flat against the ice.

"I swear to God," says the deputy, "you must be freezing half to death."

"I'm fine," she assures him. And she shuts her eyes.

Thirty-six years later, on a jet above the North Atlantic, the pilot's voice comes over the intercom, letting her know to expect a little turbulence up ahead and that she should probably fasten her seat belt.

She blinks.

Deep below the frozen surface of the Scituate Reservoir, something is waking up. It's come a very long way only to crash and find itself mired at the bottom of a lake, but something went wrong in orbit, some slight miscalculation or malfunction. Everyone makes mistakes; nothing is foolproof. Immacolata senses anger, confusion, impatience. Then the deputy's radio crackles, breaking her concentration.

You are who you are . . .

The thing beneath the ice speaks with a voice like angry bees.

. . . until you aren't anymore.

It knows she's there.

And then the day slips away from her, and for a while there's nothing but the view from the Gulfstream's window, only clouds and the shimmering bluish suggestion of the ocean so very far below. She waits to fall, not from the sky, but from the tenuous strands of Now. Falling is the easiest thing in the world.

It's only a matter of remembering not to hold on.

All things are alone in time.

That is the Second Law.

And here it is a brilliantly sunny November day in southern Vermont, hardly a month after the Mexican government ended the rebellion in Veracruz and only four days before Stalin will become the undisputed leader of the Soviet Union. She spent the night in a dingy boardinghouse in Townshend, not sleeping, reading Wordsworth by lantern light, and waiting for sunrise. The night was alive with new ghosts. A week before she arrived, the West River flooded, the worst flood in Vermont history. Eighty-four people are known dead. More than twelve hundred bridges were swept away. Fuck only knows how many miles of road and railway were destroyed, how many houses and businesses, sawmills and farms. Immacolata had to make the trip over the mountains on horseback, following muddy deer paths and steep, winding hunting trails all the way up from Brattleboro. She's always been good with horses.

At eight o'clock, she pulls on her coat and felt cloche and leaves the boardinghouse with her leather Gladstone satchel. A constable accompanies Immacolata to the tin-roofed redbrick shed behind the volunteer fire department on Grafton Road, where a surly man in overalls shows her the ugly pink-skinned thing that's been pulled out of the angry, swollen waters of the West River. There's no way of knowing how far it traveled before snagging up in a jackstraw tangle of fallen logs, barbed wire, and other debris just north of town. Two teenage boys—a farrier's sons—came upon the body and told their story all about Townshend until someone had at last gone to see what it was they'd found. And what they'd found turned out to be this.

"You up from Arkham, then?" the man in overalls asks, his words mumbled around the stem of a corncob pipe.

Between the pipe and his accent, she's having trouble understanding him. "They got lady professors down there now, do they?"

"One or two," she replies, stepping nearer to the table. "It was dead when they found it?" she asks, and the constable nods and exchanges a glance with the man in overalls.

"Ayuh," says the constable. "And if it hadn't been, we'd have shot it."

"You got a husband?" the man in overalls asks, and Immacolata ignores him. But she can't help but be amused that they're both so concerned with her sex that they've hardly seemed to give a second thought to her paleness or her smoked-lens spectacles. She sets her satchel down on an edge of the table and opens it, selecting from the array of items inside a pair of rubber gloves, forceps, and a stoppered bottle of sodium phenoxide. She pulls on the gloves.

"What are you a professor of?" the man in overalls wants to know.

"A doctor of anatomy," the constable answers for her.

"That so?" the man in overalls asks.

"That's very much so," Immacolata says, speaking hardly above a whisper. It's a good-enough lie. It'll suffice until she's done here.

The thing on the table is a biologist's nightmare,

clearly belonging to no known phylum of animals. The exoskeleton and jointed limbs suggest an arthropod, while the dorsal pair of membranous appendages might almost pass for stubby wings. The anterior limbs end in claws, like those of a crab, lobster, or crayfish. At the end of what she assumes is its neck, there is a bizarre ellipsoid organ, which she takes to be the head, sprouting fleshy tendrils that remind her of the tentacles of an anemone or sea cucumber. End to end, the creature measures just over 1.5 meters.

"You know what it is?" asks the constable.

"I don't," she says, and then uses the forceps to retract a leathery flap of skin located between two of the rows of tendrils.

"Would you venture a guess?"

"I'd prefer not to," she tells him.

Beneath the flap is a sticky yellow mass, and she takes a sample, depositing it in an empty specimen bottle. Under the microscope, it'll reveal structures reminiscent of the tellospores of certain Pucciniomycetes fungi, named rusts and smuts, but the resemblance will only be of the most general sort.

"You gonna buy it?" asks the man in overalls. He takes his pipe from his mouth, and she realizes he's missing most of his front teeth.

"I wasn't planning to," she replies, returning the specimen bottle to her satchel. "With the roads out and the trains not running, there's really no way I could get it back to Massachusetts, anyway."

The man frowns, clearly disappointed, and then he returns the pipe to its place between his gums. "Ayuh," he says. "Don't suppose you could."

"After I leave, I recommend you burn it."

"Why should we do that?" asks the constable.

"Just to be safe. Better safe than sorry, right?"

She snips one of the tendrils and places it in another bottle, then proceeds to pour a few drops of the sodium phenoxide on the thing's skin. There's no reaction whatsoever, but she hadn't expected there would be.

"Old folks round here tell stories," says the constable, "yarns about demons way up in the hills, off towards Turkey Mountain." He pauses and points north.

"Stories?" says Immacolata without looking at him.

"Yes, ma'am. Things that were here a thousand years before the Indians. My grandmother, she told us those stories when I was a child. She said they could fly, and that they'd crawled outta Hell to haunt the gorges and hollers. She said, back when she was just a girl, some prospectors from Montpelier went up into those hills and were never seen again. Said sometimes the demons flew down into the towns, and that she'd seen their footprints in the snow. But she was a superstitious woman—a bit touched, if truth be told—and we never paid her tales much heed."

"Sounds as if she had quite the healthy imagination," Immacolata tells him. Of course, she's heard the stories, too, and she's read Eli Davenport's 1839 monograph collecting various oral traditions from the Green Mountains of Vermont and the White Mountains of New Hampshire, folklore that describes creatures very similar to the drowned, broken thing laid out before her. She returns everything to her bag, snaps it shut, and pulls off the rubber gloves, depositing them on the table beside the body.

"After I leave, do promise me that you'll burn it, please. Right away."

The constable scratches his chin. "What's the rush?"

"I've noticed a few stray dogs about town," she says, "and if they were to eat it, the flesh might prove poisonous. There even could be disease. Were I you, I shouldn't take any chances."

"You sure you ain't wantin' to buy it?" asks the man in overalls.

"I'm sure," she says.

Suddenly, the plane bucks and shudders around her, and Immacolata is jolted rudely back to Now. There are no highways in the sky, as a Jimmy Stewart film once warned, only these unpredictable, invisible causeways of air to hold you up or drop you, their whims as capricious as any god's. A cold front from Greenland collides with a wall of warmer, wetter weather, and here she is caught in between. Fasten your seat belts, please remain seated, and the pilot assures her they'll be out of this shortly. She checks her iPhone for messages, but there's nothing. Maybe the storm brewing out there is blocking the signal. So she turns her attention back to the window. Fourteen thousand feet below the jet, a roiling stratocumulus canyon land of thunderheads has hidden the sea from view.

Time is the navigator, and we are only hitchhikers.

The Third Law.

She slips, and the plane fades like mist coming apart at the end of morning.

For a handful of seconds, she's back in that booth in Winslow, smoking and listening as the Signalman talks about Drew Standish and his followers.

"It's all right there on the suicide drive," he says.

Then she blinks, and now Immacolata walks the streets of a city that once was Los Angeles. To those who never left, now it is merely the City, shattered by the great earthquake of 2032, flooded, burned, and finally consumed by the invaders who came first as a terrible wasting disease carried by windborne alien spores. It's not as if there weren't warnings. She stops outside a crumbling building, gutted by decay and half buried beneath the glistening, ropy fungi that grows almost everywhere. She knows this place; she's been here several times before.

The sun never shines on the City.

The black ships have seen to that.

Two weeks ago, the Pan-Asian Alliance dropped nuclear warheads all across southern India, from Thiruvananthapuram to Bangalore, in a desperate, last ditch to halt the northward progression of the invaders. Three days from now, the titular head of what remains of the United States will be assassinated by militants from the Earth-Yuggoth Cooperative. Afterwards, the EYC will burn what little is left of Washington D.C.

There are signposts in the future, just as there are signposts in the past.

A traveler can get lost here, too, easy as pie.

A young woman is standing in the doorway of the building, and she waves to Immacolata. Whatever this place once was—perhaps a hotel, perhaps a bank or office building—now it's a filthy burrow where the blighted and dying huddle together and wait for the end. It's been seven years since the last evacuation, and the borders were sealed long ago. The bridges blown, the highways mined. Dozens of snipers guard the perimeter day and night, making sure no one will ever get out of the ruins of L.A. Not that most here would ever try to leave. These women and men were not so much abandoned, as they allowed themselves to be left behind. Some might say that these are the resigned, the ones who saw the writing on the wall.

The New Gods rule here, the Elder Beings.

Everything old is new again.

The woman in the doorway beckons. She tries to smile, but her twisted face only vaguely remembers how, and the expression comes off more like a grimace.

"You came back," she says. Her voice is hoarse and phlegmy.

"I did," Immacolata replies, her own voice muffled by the mask and rebreather she's wearing. "I said I would."

"I was afraid we'd seen the last of you. I didn't want to believe that, but I was starting to, all the same."

Immacolata is carrying a backpack bulging with canned goods, mostly fruit and vegetables, and she lays it at the woman's feet.

"I wish I could've brought more. But—"

"This is plenty. You do so much for us. Don't you dare ever apologize for not doing more. We get by."

But Immacolata has seen what passes for getting by with the inhabitants of the City. She's followed them into the sewer and subway tunnels where they hunt coyotes, feral cats and dogs, rats and swarms of roaches. All these species have long since become subterranean dwellers, driven mad by the spores, their morphology transformed, mutated by the mycelial mats and fruiting bodies rooted in bone and muscle, blood and skin, running rampant through every internal organ. As with the people who hunt them, some are hardly recognizable for what they once were.

The woman unzips the backpack and takes out a dented can of peaches. "Oh," she says. "I remember these. We ate these when I was a child."

There's a symbol painted above the doorway. It identifies those living in the building as supplicants of Nyarlathotep and Azathoth. Whether or not they truly are, whether they regularly make the trek to the temple a few blocks way, that's another matter altogether. The mark's enough to keep the ravagers at bay, the shuffling heaps who prowl the streets and alleyways searching for the faithless. Immacolata has seen the crucifixions for herself.

"And pears," the woman says, pulling out another can. "I remember these, too."

Then Immacolata smells ozone and gasoline, and she looks up just as the cloud of invaders appears, seventy-five, a hundred, a living veil skimming low above rooftops, somehow staying aloft with those thick, stubby wings. They're identical to the drowned creature she glimpsed in a storage shed in Townshend, Vermont, in November 1927. After only a few seconds, the buzzing becomes just short of deafening, and the woman grabs

Immacolata's left elbow, yanking her roughly toward the darkness waiting inside the building.

"Come on. We can't stay out here. They won't follow us. They never follow us."

The woman leads her through the lobby, then down a steeply slanting hallway and past the deeper, gaping blackness of twin elevator shafts. In here, the droning calls of the invaders are muffled, made distant by thick stone walls, and Immacolata is surprised at her own relief. Their language works its way into your brain, digging in and lodging in the convolutions of the cerebrum, burrowing into the fine grooves of the cerebellum, threatening to highjack all reason and even the basest animal instincts. She's led down a crooked flight of stairs to the basement level.

To the garden.

"They'll be gone soon," the woman assures her. "They'll pass us by. They always do."

It isn't dark down here. There's a violet-blue phosphorescence cast by things that can no longer, even by the broadest of definitions, be called human. They seem to have sprouted directly from the concrete floor, anchored motionless for months or even years. Some have grown one into another, all pretenses at individuality abandoned. Here and there, Immacolata can discern the dim suggestion of limbs and faces. The worst are the ones who still have eyes and mouths, the ones who watch her and struggle to speak.

"It won't be long. You'll see," the woman says, oblivious to the horrors around them.

You are who you are, until you aren't anymore.

Immacolata Sexton, dead and undying child of another age, blinks.

"The World," she said to the Signalman. "The dancer is meant to signify the final attainment of man, a merging of the self-conscious with the unconscious and a blending of those two states with the superconscious."

Again she falls, which is the easiest thing to do. Swept up by bottomless, billowing darkness, she tumbles.

The World implies the ultimate state of cosmic awareness, the final goal . . .

Der Übergeist.

The darkness comes apart.

And the buzzing is replaced by the comforting hum of the Gulfstream's engines. She rubs at her eyes, then checks her watch. Almost a full hour and a half passed that time. Nearly too long, and she's well aware how much she's pushing the margin of safety. Outside, the summer sun is sinking quickly towards the sea. In another moment, the pilot announces they're approaching Ireland.

8.

Not Yet Explored
(July 4, 2015)

ANYONE WOULD HAVE TO admit it's a neat trick, Immacolata Sexton's knack for mentally slipping the surly bonds of Grandfather Time to touch the face of Eternity, all those Immacolatas that have been and are yet to come, even if she's not quite genuinely "unstuck." She's no Billy Pilgrim, true enough. But, all the same, take a page from her playbook. Because it may be we have gotten ahead of ourselves, which is always a danger when attempting to perceive the apparent progression of any series of events as orderly, strung like pearls on a silken thread. In imposing order, it's easy to miss the obvious.

Look over your shoulder. Become the wife of Lot.

A pillar of salt, enlightened.

At 1:54 P.M. EDT, one day after the Signalman entered a ranch house near the shore of the Salton Sea, the mission operations center at Johns Hopkins Applied Physics Laboratory abruptly lost contact with NASA's interplanetary probe *New Horizons*. Autopilot switched the craft from its main computer to a backup and placed the probe in safe mode, then began attempts to reestablish communications with Earth. Using the Deep Space Network in California, Madrid, and Canberra, NASA reestablished contact at 3:15 P.M. But a lot can happen in an hour and twenty-one minutes, especially when you're three billion miles away and it takes roughly nine hours to phone home. At 4 P.M., the New Horizons Anomaly Review Board met to "gather information on the problem and initiate a recovery plan." A software glitch was discovered, a timing flaw in the command sequence that would allow the probe's Pluto flyby. While the Signalman and everyone else who'd entered Drew Standish's compound waited out their time in quarantine, while what they found there was removed from the scene and transported via five unmarked, refrigerated semitrailer trucks to the USAF facility most commonly known as Area 51, engineers worked to resolve the problem.

In Albany, New York, in the subbasement of the Erastus Corning Tower, all of this was duly noted, and correlations were quickly drawn between the grisly discovery at Moonlight Ranch and the ailing spacecraft. Nothing escapes the all-seeing gaze of Albany, except, of course, when it does. Vermont in November 1927, for example.

Tiddley-pom.

And so it goes.

We move on to the matter of a secret history.

Ten days from its closest approach to Pluto, *New Horizons* passed less than one hundred miles from what might, for the sake of convenience, be described as a cloud. A thousand times denser than the hard vacuum surrounding it and as wide as the Mediterranean Sea, it squatted in the path of the probe. Deep inside its heart, electrical impulses raced along an intricate maze of hydrocarbon dendrites and axons, relaying detailed observations of *New Horizons,* building a profile of this strange visitor from the inner solar system. Without eyes, it saw. Without hands, it touched. Launched ten millennia ago from a dwarf planet far beyond the orbit of Pluto, the cloud has waited, patiently, for this encounter. Here, in this moment, is its purpose fulfilled. The cloud is a voyager, too.

In 1933, both James Whale and Edgar Rice Burroughs dreamt of the cloud.

In 1945, an actor who'd once played a hero determined to rescue an imperiled alien princess also dreamt of it. A few months later, it was the last thing on his mind before he died of a heart attack.

In 1971, three astronomers at the Lawrence Livermore National Laboratory, all engaged in a search for a hypothesized "Planet X," repeatedly suffered nightmares of a cloud from deep space that swallowed the world. Writing in his private journal, one of these men referred to the monstrous cloud as Jörmungandr.

In 2009, Drew Standish turned a page in an ancient, wicked book (we will say that a book can *be* wicked) and read a description of the cloud penned three and a half centuries before the birth of Christ. The book named the cloud, though it's a name that Standish has never dared to speak out loud. He knows the cloud is a harbinger. He knows the cloud is an angel with a golden trumpet. He knows the cloud guards the gates of Eden.

Six years later, it sent a message that briefly shut down *New Horizons,* and a billion miles farther out than Pluto, buzzing fungal things in black towers hunched over their own machines, receiving and analyzing everything the cloud saw.

What rough beast, indeed.

These things happen.

And these.

And these.

9.

The Puppet Motel
(July 11, 2015)

EVERYTHING FOR MILES AROUND has post-apocalyptic cowboy movie names. If John Wayne had been a spook, he'd have thought of names like these. Flying in low, the Signalman ticks them off: Jumbled Hills, Mercury, Yucca Flats, Fallout Hills and the Paradise Range, Tikaboo Valley, Papoose Lake, Sedan Crater. It's better than thinking about what-the-fuck-ever is waiting for him down below. The Janet airlines Boeing 737-600, dirty white with that crimson cheatline slash just for emphasis, begins its final descent, dropping towards a landscape so desolate and scorched that God's own nuclear arsenal must have been called in for the job. To the north he can see the paler playa expanse of Groom Lake proper, a funny name for something that last held water ten thousand years ago. He's been told that whenever it rains, tiny shrimplike bugs called copepods wriggle their way up from the salty clay, shaking off dormancy, only to be devoured by hungry flocks of seagulls that fly in all the way from California for the feast. The plight of the copepods, thinks the Signalman, is a pretty good metaphor for every goddamn thing about Area 51 and, for that matter, every goddamn thing about his life.

Five more minutes and they're on the ground, and the dingy Boeing—purchased cheap from Air China—is taxying towards the terminal. This is the first time he's flown since 1995, the same year this plane rolled off the assembly line. He waits until it has come to a complete stop, and then he waits almost five minutes more before unfastening his seat belt and retrieving Immacolata's briefcase from the overhead compartment.

Back on the train, Jack Dunaway kept eyeing the briefcase like it was a rattlesnake coiled and waiting to strike.

"How much less of a mess would we be in," he asked, "if those Limey sons of bitches hadn't spent the last hundred years keeping us in the dark?"

"She's not a Brit," said the Signalman. "She was born in Tennessee. At least, that's what they say."

"I didn't mean her," said Dunaway. "Well, I didn't mean only her. I didn't mean her in particular."

"Ain't no point in getting pissy because the other side's better than us at lying, cheating, and burying the truth. She does her job, just the fuck like you."

"Whose side are you on, anyway?"

And the Signalman almost asked, *You really think that's how it works, us against them? You really gonna berate me for not cheering on the home team?* But Dunaway is exactly the sort of douchebag who tries to advance in the Company by ratting out his betters. Joe McCarthy would have loved the guy. The Signalman keeps his questions to himself.

"They're cooperating now," he says instead.

"Sure they are. Now that they're scared. Now that it's too late."

"There, there, Little Buckaroo. We're not talking doomsday. Not just yet. Anyhow, where would we be if Y hadn't shown a little mercy and left us the prize back in '78? Not like they had to. Credit where credit's due and all that."

"Credit? We should have nailed them to the wall just for showing up in Rhode Island, never mind sending two of our agents on a wild goose chase so Barbican could snatch the right of first refusal."

"And you think I'm the one with anger problems," the Signalman said, and poured himself another shot of J&B.

The exit door opens, letting in the desert heat, letting in the terra-cotta light of the fading afternoon, and he makes his way along the narrow aisle, then down the foldout airstairs and onto the cracked tarmac. There's no one waiting to meet him, but he hadn't really expected there would be. The Signalman's not exactly the sort of errand boy who rates a welcoming committee. He'd hoped there might be time for a shower, a quick bite to eat, maybe another drink before the party begins. And if wishes were horses, he'd still be on that train. He flashes his credentials for a couple of bored guards, and they let him pass. Neither of them looks him in the eye or says a word. It's usually like that, when security sees a red shield, especially if it's their first time. For most of these guys, Albany's little more than a black-budget fairy tale, an intelligence community urban legend, until you're face-to-face with the undeniable fact of it.

Cut to the chase. Get on with it, already.

They're holding her in Zone 17, and that means a short ride on Dreamland's very own underground maglev. There's a whole goddamn city down here, a rat's maze of tunnels and bunkers, substations, railways, and maintenance shafts, two dozen layers stacked one atop the other like a birthday cake. This is the beating heart and mind of the base, safe from satellites and Google Earth, hidden from the UFO and conspiracy nuts who lurk about the perimeters with their cameras and telephoto lenses.

The Signalman dislikes being below almost as much as he dislikes flying.

But this is where they've brought her, so this is where he goes.

Her name is Chloe Stringfellow, and she was the last of Standish's fourteen unfortunate recruits, the one most recently infected, the least advanced case. She's also the only one of the bunch considered a survivor, though that's not going to last. He's been told that she has a few hours left, maybe less; she isn't likely to make it until morning. He's also been told that she's scared, and if he's lucky, that'll work in his favor.

The laboratory smells of ammonia and recycled air. There are two men in white coats who show him to the containment cell. He'd hesitate to call them doctors.

The merciless glare of fluorescents has erased every trace of shadow.

"We've got her on a cocktail of dimethylamylamine and amphetamine," one of them tells the Signalman. "We're doing our best to keep her lucid, but whatever this pathogen is, it's acting as a powerful hypnotic."

"If I were you," says the other, "I'd hurry."

Her cell is fronted by a thick sheet of Plexiglas, and there's a metal folding chair parked in front of it, waiting for him. Inside, she's sitting in an identical chair, head bowed, shoulders slumped, staring at her open palms. He takes his seat, and one of the men in white coats switches on an intercom. The Signalman's seen the corpses of people who've died of Ebola, leprosy, radiation poisoning, not to mention any number of biological and chemical weapons. But somehow this is worse. Maybe it's because she's still alive.

"Chloe," he says, his voice rendered flat and tinny by the intercom, "I need to talk with you. I know that's probably the very last thing you want to do right now, but unless you cooperate, I can't guarantee my bosses are ever going to let you leave this place. Unless you help me, I can't even guarantee they're going to keep treating you. They let people die. I need you to understand that, Chloe. The men and women I work for, they let people die all the time."

"I've seen you before," she says without looking at him, and her voice is as raw as uncooked hamburger. "At the ranch. You're one of them."

"Yeah. That's right. I'm one of them. But I want to help you. I really do, and I can't unless you're willing to help me."

"You don't know what I've done," she says. "None of you. You don't have any idea what I've done. You couldn't imagine."

"Then how about you give me a hand with that?"

She laughs, and he thinks it's one of the worst sounds in the world, that laugh.

"I want some water," she tells him. "They won't even give me a drink of water. I asked over and over again. I told them how thirsty I am, but they won't listen."

The Signalman glances at the men in white coats, and

the one who told him to hurry shakes his head. When he turns back to the girl, she's looking at him. Her eyes are the color of gangrene.

"Answer a few questions for me," he says. "You do that, and I'll see you get whatever you want. Water, a Coke, iced tea, whatever the hell you'd like."

"My throat is so dry," she replies.

"Where is he?"

"Where is who?"

"Standish. Where is Drew Standish."

She narrows those rotting eyes, then goes back to staring at her hands.

"Where are the others?" she wants to know. "Did you bring them here, too? You're not cops, are you?"

"No, I'm not a cop. And the others are here, not far away."

"It isn't fair," she says. "I'm his favorite. As soon as he found me, I was his favorite. Madeline said so. It isn't fair that they'd go before me."

"Who's Madeline?"

"It isn't fair at all."

"Was she still at the ranch when we got there?"

"No," the girl answers. "Madeline is the Sixteenth Trump. Madeline is the Tower. She went with him. She left me to watch over the others, and she went with him."

"And where did he go? Where is he now?"

"Are they dead?" she asks him. "Did I kill them?"

The Signalman hesitates, weighing his lies, weighing consequences.

"I don't think that I meant to kill them," says Chloe Stringfellow. "I was angry, that's all. I kept waiting for the television to call *my* name, but it was too busy talking to them. Like I wasn't even in the room. Like maybe he'd made a mistake, bringing me there, and I was just some sort of accident. But that can't be. Drew said, 'You are the path unto deliverance. There are no accidents here.'"

"What if he lied to you? Have you thought of that? You have to have considered that possibility."

She shakes her head very slowly, shrugs her shoulders, and licks at her lips. It seems to him as if her every movement requires tremendous effort, some force of will that's almost beyond her.

"You have, haven't you? In fact, that's what you're thinking right now, that maybe none of it was true. That maybe he used you. Maybe he used all of you."

"No," she says, so quietly that he almost misses it, and she shakes her head again.

"Why are you still protecting him, Chloe? That's what I want to know. Look what he's done to you. You trusted him, and he's betrayed that trust. He left you there in that house to die. He got cold feet, and he ran. He left you—all of you—behind."

"No," she says. "Drew *saved* me. If anyone's a traitor, it's me, not him."

The Signalman leans forward, resting his elbows on the knees of his cheap suit. "Your were abandoned," he says. "Is that how our saviors treat us?"

"If you could have seen me before—"

"Are you really expecting me to believe you were worse off than you are now? This thing is eating you alive, you know that, right? It's using you, just like Standish used you, taking what you are and changing you into something it needs. He isn't a shaman, and this isn't divine transformation. It's a disease. A parasite."

"You haven't seen what I've seen."

"That's right, and I don't fucking *need* to," the Signalman replies. There's anger in his voice, bright and violent, that he'd not intended to show. It's too early in the game for that. If he isn't careful, he'll blow the pantomime and lose her.

Don't fool yourself. You've already lost her.

She looks up again, and whatever he was going to say next, he lets it go. There's an ugly swelling on the left side of her face that wasn't there a minute ago. The skin is taut, shiny, ready to split open.

The fungus spreads through an ant's body, maturing inside its head—and this is where things really get interesting.

"You didn't come here to help me," she says. "You're

frightened. He told us, all the world will be frightened, until they understand. Fear is an affront to the messengers, and the heart of the passage is a release from the prison of our fears."

"You were better off on heroin," he replies. "At least it never promised you anything it couldn't deliver."

Chloe shuts her eyes, and she manages a crooked sort of smile.

"I wish you could see," she sighs. "I wish I could show you."

"Her BP is dropping," says one of the white-coated men, his voice calm and smooth as vanilla ice cream, like the bastard sees this shit every damn day of the week. "Her body temperature, too."

"Is she on anything for the pain?" the Signalman asks.

"No. Only the stimulants. Our orders were very specific on that point."

"It doesn't hurt," she says, right on cue. "It doesn't hurt at all."

"She's probably telling the truth," says the other white-coated man. "The pathogen seems to be producing a compound that acts as a neurotransmitter and mimics endorphins, pretty much the same as morphine."

Behind the Plexiglas, the girl lifts her right arm, and she points at the briefcase. The Signalman set it on the floor beside the metal folding chair. For the first time in more than twenty-four hours, he'd forgotten all about it.

"I know what's in there," she says, slurring her words. "The gift of Babylon the Great, Mother of All Prostitutes and Obscenities in the World. The lies by which she would deceive every living soul. He told us she was coming. He told us about her, about the diner in Arizona, about the filthy whore seducing you, hiding herself behind that name. The Immaculate Protector, the Sacristan. But you're such a clever one. Surely you can see behind the demon's mask."

"We're running out of time," says the Signalman, speaking to Chloe Stringfellow or the men in white coats or only to himself.

"And you," she murmurs, "you're the Twelfth Trump, the Hanged Man. You don't know it yet, but you are. *Pittura infamante,* dangling by one ankle from a withered gallows tree. Babylon didn't put you there, no, but she pulled the knots of that fylfot cross so much tighter than they'd ever been pulled before."

The bulge on her cheek has turned a livid red and has grown until it's almost as large as a tennis ball. She scratches at it, and the Signalman wants to believe he only imagines the movement beneath her skin.

"You dance for her, dangling," she says, only it's not *her* voice any longer. But it's a voice he's heard before, on a CD from Immacolata's briefcase. It's the voice of the man she's given her life for.

"Who am I talking to?" he asks.

"You," says a man talking through the dying girl, ignoring the Signalman's question, "you dance for her, hanging, her long black hair drawn out tightly, fiddling whisper music on those strings. And bats with baby faces . . ." But the voice trails off then, and the girl's body shudders violently. She slips off the chair to the floor.

"She's flatlining," says one of the men in white lab coats.

"We need to shut this down," says the other. "It's over."

And the Signalman is up and on his feet then, suddenly more afraid and more confused than he's been in a very long time, even more than he was at the ranch by the Salton Sea, when he stepped into the room filled with the smell of mushrooms and the insectile drone of television static. When he first saw Chloe Stringfellow, standing over what was left of her thirteen companions, a shotgun cradled in the crook of one arm. Whatever's happening in the cell, it's nothing he expected, nothing he was warned *could* happen. If Y knew, it's something they've kept from him. He steps forward and places his right hand flat against the Plexiglas divider.

"You talk to me," he growls. "You stop playing games, you son of a bitch, and you *talk* to me right this goddamn minute."

"Don't be a sore loser," Drew Standish whispers, and then the bulge on the girl's face bursts, a few seconds before that side of her head entirely collapses in upon itself, spilling a cloud of fine mustard-colored spores. An alarm goes off, and the fluorescents are replaced by crimson light that pulses like the ache of a broken bone. Something pulls itself free of Chloe Stringfellow's chest and begins to roll slowly away.

"I'm sorry," one of the white-coated men tells him, sounding not the least bit sorry. "We can't wait any longer. Containment protocol." And then cryogenic vents tucked into the ceiling above the fruiting corpse slide open and release jets of liquid nitrogen, flash freezing the nightmare in the cell.

This is the way the world ends.

Tiddley-pom.

10.

The Rapture as Low Burlesque
(July 3, 2015)

THIS IS THE MORNING that I have been promised. I open my eyes from a dream that seems more real and brighter and louder than any waking memory, and dimly I recall that this is *the* morning. I lie in my bunk and watch a galaxy of dust motes sifting through a shaft of sunlight, here on the 6,997th day since my birth to a woman whose face I can now hardly even recall. The mother of my body, the mother of my captivity. *Chloe, you were such a beautiful, beautiful baby. I thought you were a gift from the angels, and I couldn't imagine what I had possibly done to have deserved you.* I stare at that shaft of light, slipping in through the tattered drapes, and the dream of the home that was never home slowly begins to fray, admitting this day, instead. This day, 6,977 days after I was shat out, mewling and soft, into a gallery of daggers and broken glass. I wish Drew had been there with me, in the dream. I wish he could have spoken to my mother, and then she could have prepared me for *this* day. She would have known what I was made for. I might never have strayed from the path, seduced by the ways of wolves and smack and hypodermic solace. I might never have become someone who needed to be cut free from the belly of the beast.

The air stirs, and the dust motes swirl.

I'd thought that there would be pain when this morning arrived, but there's almost no pain at all. My mouth tastes like the air in a cellar. And my head is filled with bees.

I should get up. I should get up and go find the others.

Last night, Drew drove me down to Bombay Beach, and we sat in his car and listened to the engine cooling and the desert cooling and the black expanse of Jachin breathing in and out, out and in. We parked at the shore, near the rusting shell of an old school bus sunk almost up to its windows in the salt and the evaporite muck and the bones of dead tilapia and pelicans. He sipped vodka from a paper bag, and he watched my eyes while I watched the starlight pinpoints shimmering above the sea.

"What do you espy away up there, little Chloe?"

"I see fire," I told him. It was the truth. "I see black fire that's been burning almost forever, and I see the spheres that move through the flames. I see the tiny boat we've launched, and I see that *other* boat, sailing out to meet us halfway."

He smiled, and then he laughed a small laugh. And that's when I remembered Madeline was sitting in the backseat. She lit a cigarette, and for a few moments the night smelled less like dead fish and brine and more like matches.

"You see all that?" she asked.

"Yeah," I said. I'm not afraid of Madeline, but sometimes I have thought that she wishes Drew had never found me in that alleyway. I think, maybe, she's decided I've come to steal away her Titan for my own.

"What else do you see, little Chloe?" Drew asked.

"Towers, I see towers. Like an old movie about Ali Baba and the Forty Thieves or Sinbad the Sailor. A city of spiraling towers and crystal domes, a city in a desert of ebony sand, a desert at the edge of an ocean. But it's not like any ocean we know. There aren't any waves. There aren't tides. It's as flat and still as a mirror, Drew. It's as flat and still as glass. And it isn't water, either. It's an ocean of methane, ethane, propane. Sometimes, I see mighty storms that march furiously across that ocean and march across the ebony desert and bury the city beneath blizzards of benzene snow." And I wonder at the words falling from my lips, because I comprehend they're not precisely, not entirely, my own. I am a vessel, prepared for a new purpose, and the messengers are free to speak through me. My eyes, my brain, my mouth, but the messengers are translators, intermediaries weaving my dumbstruck thoughts into the tapestry that Drew needs to hear.

For I have gazed in sleep,
On things my memory scarce can keep. . . .

"You're my little poet," he said, then turns on the car radio. There's a Beatles song playing, and I know that Drew knew there would be.

In the backseat, Madeline made a sound that I might only mistake for derisive.

"Am I awake?" I asked.

"Love," he said, "that's nothing you should ever worry yourself about again. Waking and sleeping, you've found your way through the Cavern of Flame, and now you stand at the top of the Seven Hundred Steps. For you, the distinction between dream and waking thought has begun to implode, folding in upon itself. You've become a singularity to dissolve everything that separates the one from the other."

And then he asked me to tell them a story, he and Madeline, and so I told him the story about the princess in her onyx tower and the Sword Forged of Lamentation and the tall, pale woman who was her lover and then became her champion. I told them about the dragon at the gate and the whisperers below the mountains.

I should get up. It's hot, and it must be very late morning by now. It would be so easy to lie here in the sweltering day, even though my anxious excitement tugs at my belly, at the very centermost parts of me. The others will be waiting. Drew and Madeline left before dawn, and now it all falls to me. Now it all falls *on* me. I have been entrusted with the future, and here I am lying in bed half the damn day, getting turned around in my thoughts when there's so much still to be done. I sit up, and the alarm clock across the room says that it's only 8:47, and I breathe a grateful sigh of relief.

The house is quieter than it's ever been.

"What if I'm not ready?" I asked Drew the night before, sitting there by the sea in his little red wagon, and he laughed and kissed my cheek.

"You're ready," he said. "You're more ready than you can imagine."

But you won't be the first.

And my head jerked around then, as if I'd been stung, as if a bee or a wasp had slipped up my T-shirt and stung me in some especially vulnerable spot. I stared back over my shoulder at Madeline and the soft glow of her cigarette. But she was watching the sky, not me. And she hadn't said a word.

"It's okay," said Drew. "In all the wide, wide universe,

there's no one in whom I have more faith than you."

They'll go before you, the thirteen, one by one by one, and you will only be an afterthought, dragged along in their wake. Tardy. Almost forgotten.

Madeline tapped ash on the floorboard, and Drew asked me to finish my story. It would be the last story I'd ever tell him, and he wanted to hear all the way to the end.

> And as I look, I fain would know
> The paths whereon thy dream-steps go,
> The spectral realms that thou canst see
> With eyes veiled from the world and me.

I never imagined a house could be this quiet.

My sweat has stained the sheets yellow, and I push them onto the floor. It's not the first time I've seen that stain, but it's the first time it's ever struck me as unclean. I lean over and shove the dirty sheet beneath the bed, only half understanding that what I feel is not only revulsion, but shame, too. Like waking from a dream of bleeding to the shock of my first period and rose petals spread across the linen.

No. Never mind. Not like that at all.

I get to my feet, going slowly because the dizziness is worse this morning. No surprise there. I knew it would be. There should be no surprises whatsoever today. It's all dot to dot, paint by number from here. This map before me is not terra incognita; I only have to fill in the blanks, and I've spent months learning the answers. I was *born* knowing the answers, 6,997 days ago, but must have been so terrified at the truth of it all that I did my best to forget. That was the road to an alleyway between Ninety-third and Ninety-fourth streets in Westmont, desolation row, detonation boulevard, the road of needles, the fucking path of least resistance. The Coward's Way. But the willful scales fell from my eyes on the road to my own private Damascus, Drew's Damascus, the television white-noise Damascus where the messengers sing from cathode ray tubes. One foot in front of the other. That's all it takes. Go to the thirteen, now, and be sure everything is just exactly as it ought to be. You're the fourteenth, and you're also the midwife. There can be no greater honor, can there? Make certain that each crosses at her or his appointed time, that they all bloom and spread themselves to the winds blowing down from the Chocolate Mountains, the *star* winds, the mighty Coachella sirocco. And only when each has folded open may I sit down and follow their examples.

The very last, I hear Madeline whisper. *By the time you arrive, little afterthought, the deed will be done. The parade will have come and gone. But don't be sad. Every revolution needs a rear guard, just in case. Someone will be thankful, I'm sure.*

In the hallway, between the kitchen and the television room, that's when I see the shotgun. It's always been there, the break-top double-barrel twelve-gauge that Drew said he got cheap off some bikers up in San Bernardino. To keep away the coyotes, he said, though I've never seen a coyote come anywhere near Moonlight Ranch. I don't know what the fuck they'd even eat out here. I've never even seen a jackrabbit or an armadillo, either, and it's not like coyotes can eat creosote bushes or cacti. I check to see if the shotgun's loaded, pushing back the latch to open the breech. I can't recollect just when I learned to do that. But maybe Drew taught me, right after I came here. In case there *were* coyotes. I find two shells in the gun, and didn't Madeline tell me there were more in a kitchen cupboard?

What are you doing, Chloe? What the fuck do you think you're doing?

I find the extra shells, and I carry the gun with me when I go to the television room. All the others, they're too far along for the bunks, and so they've slept here, bathed in the salt-and-pepper light of the television, wrapped in the lullaby voices buried deep in the static since the Big Bang was new. My 6,997 days, the cosmos's 13.7 billion years, this planet's 4.5 billion years. I never used to have a head for facts and figures, but the messengers have brought so, so many gifts.

The room is becoming a garden, and it's my job to see that the flowers open out of doors, not inside this stifling room. They would be wasted here. What good is a rose that no one ever sees or smells.

What are you doing?

I won't even remember pulling the trigger. I know that. I am absolutely certain of that, just as I'm certain that I'll also have no doubt whatsoever that I did. It isn't fair that I should be the last, not when I'm his favorite. I know that, and Madeline knows, too. *It was always a part of his plan,* she whispers behind my eyes. *But not a part that even he fully understands. It's like that, you know. Sometimes even prophets need a helping hand. Just like Judas helped Jesus. Maybe you've never been a Christian, never gone to church or prayed, but I bet you know that story, I bet you understand that analogy. So don't you worry your pretty head. You won't be last, after all.*

It wouldn't have been fair.

I find them all right where they ought to be, and the gun cracks the day like an egg.

11.

Lowdown Subterranean End-Times Blues (Revisited)

THE HAUNTED HUMAN PSYCHE craves resolution. Indeed, it petulantly demands it. This unfortunate state of affairs may be a simple issue of how gray matter has been hardwired by millions of years of mutation and natural selection, a quirk of evolution riding piggyback on the emergence of a complex higher consciousness. We cannot know if the australopithecines or their forebears were burdened by this same weakness—and it *is* a weakness—as we cannot observe their interactions with an unresolved and likely unresolvable universe. We can't question them. But humans, inherent problem solvers that we are, chafe at problems that cannot be solved, questions that cannot ever, once and for all, satisfactorily be put to rest: the assassination of President Kennedy, the Permian–Triassic extinction event, the Wow! signal, Casper Hauser, the Voynich manuscript, the identity of Jack the Ripper. Just for example.

How many angels can dance on the head of a pin?

I got a million of 'em. The mind balks at the idea that these mysteries will never be solved. Which, of course, has no bearing on their solvability. All the king's horses and all the king's men are for naught.

Wishing ain't getting.

In his heart of hearts, the Signalman knows this is gospel. But his job is, all the same, to pursue answers for the Powers That Be, the powerbrokers, the gatekeepers. And in the absence of answers, he's learned to settle for the doubtful consolation of necessary fictions. He is, above all else, a practical man. Whatever idealism he once might have harbored was sacrificed a long, long time ago. Scar tissue stiffens and numbs the inquisitorial soul.

The "death" of Chloe Stringfellow closed avenues of investigation that can never again be opened.

And the answers in Immacolata Sexton's dreadful briefcase only get him just so far.

And so it goes.

Still, and all, there is a trail of half truths and three-quarter lies that leads him, finally, to San Diego and the Hollister Street Days Inn, less than three miles from the Mexican border, less than a hundred miles from the ranch on the shores of the Salton Sea. He caught a lucky break, got a tip from a CI, a schizophrenic who's spent the last two decades creating a concordance for the *Weekly World News,* "the World's Only Reliable News," painstakingly cataloging and correlating everything from Jersey Devil sightings to Bat Boy, from Israeli mermaids to the discovery of an alien spacecraft at the bottom of the Baltic Sea. Even a broken clock is right twice a day, and patterns inevitably emerge. *All those strange things that come and go as early warnings.* And one of those patterns leads the Signalman and three FBI agents to Room 210.

That the tip came from the lunatic fringe and not from complaints about the smell is just exactly the sort of thing that never ceases to amaze the Signalman.

There in the parking lot was Drew Standish's 1967 red Buick Sport Wagon, and behind the door to Room 210 was his corpse and the corpse of a woman who will later be identified as Madeline Nightlinger, a former Facebook executive who'd been missing since January 2013. A coroner back at Groom Lake will determine that they'd both been dead since at least July 5. Their skulls have been cut open and their brains removed, the brain stem so neatly divided from the spinal column that even the most jaded neurosurgeon would surely be impressed. There was not so much as a drop of blood anywhere. The bodies have been positioned on their backs, hands folded on their chests. Both were naked, their clothing neatly folded and placed thoughtfully in the room's chest of drawers. As for the top halves of their bisected crania, genuine skullcaps, those turned up in the bathroom sink. Hungry ants were everywhere.

The brains themselves were nowhere to be found.

One of the FBI agents excused himself and vomited his breakfast over the railing and onto the asphalt below.

Standish's Black Book, described in a dossier from Immacolata's briefcase, was nowhere to be found. On the other hand, there was a peculiar metal cylinder resting on a table near the door, and some would say that it more than makes up for the missing book. The Signalman is, however, most emphatically not one of those people. The cylinder only poses a hundred new questions and answers none. It's about a foot tall, not quite a foot in diameter, with three sockets arranged in an isosceles triangle on the convex surface of one end. As for the composition of the metal itself, that will never be determined, though it will be found to match other anomalous samples recovered from Roswell, New Mexico, and Kecksburg, Pennsylvania. SEM magnifications from $< 100\times - 15,000\times$, ED$\times$ area scans, elemental mapping, and point-and-shoot analysis will all fail to yield conclusive results.

Looking at the cylinder, the Signalman shuddered, and he considered, albeit briefly, chartering a fishing boat and sinking the damned thing in the deep Pacific water out beyond the Coronado Escarpment. In the long years to come, the cowardice that stays his hand will be a recurring source of regret. Could'a, should'a, would'a.

Don't you know it.

Three nights after the discovery at the Days Inn, when Standish and Nightlinger's corpses are safely on ice in Nevada and the metal cylinder has forever vanished into the labyrinthine bowels of Dreamland, the Signalman—more than half drunk—gives in and calls a number that Immacolata Sexton gave him that night back in Winslow, scribbled on the back of a coffee-stained paper napkin. He'd almost thrown it in the trash; he'd certainly never intended to use it. Not for Sweet Baby Jesus, love, or green folding money. But in the dead of night, alone with his thoughts and memories and fears, alone with a deeper despair than he's ever known, intentions turn out to mean less than nothing. She answers on the fourth ring. Her voice is every bit as icy as he remembers.

"You found him," she says before he has a chance to even say hello.

"How the fuck do you know that?"

"A little bird," she replies.

"Whatever," he says, and laughs. "I'm calling it quits, putting in for early retirement. I think they'll let me go. I think Albany sees they've wrung every last bit out of me they're going to get. The salad days are over and gone."

There's a long pause then, and it's the Signalman who finally breaks the silence.

"It's not finished, is it?"

"No," she says. "It isn't. It's only just begun." But she kindly doesn't tell him about the streets she'll walk in a ruined L.A. only twenty-eight years farther along, or the battalions of winged fungoid monstrosities skimming low above shattered skyscrapers, or the black ships.

"You know about *New Horizons,* too?"

"I do."

"Good," he says. "Then I don't have to tell you."

"If it's any consolation, you did the best you could. And you may have bought us all a little more time."

Another pause, and then he says, "That tarot card, the one we found nailed to the front door of the ranch house—"

"The World."

"Yeah, the World. You're the dancer, aren't you?"

He listens and waits while she lights a cigarette.

"No more than anyone else," she says. "No more than you. No more than that poor Stringfellow girl or Standish or the woman who served us coffee that night in Arizona."

"Did you keep the card?"

"No. It's in the archives at Barbican. For safekeeping."

He goes to the refrigerator for a few ice cubes, cracks the seal on a fresh bottle of J&B, and refills his glass. "Would you like to know a secret," he asks.

"Sure. What's one more, after all."

"That night, they wanted me to kill you. They wanted me to kill you and take the briefcase. I talked them out of it. I still don't really know why, but I talked them out of it."

"Yes," she says, "I know. No hard feelings. No ill will."

He asks her another couple of questions, though they're really nothing of consequence, and then she hangs up first. He'll catch hell from Albany for making the call, but what the fuck. He only wishes it had left him feeling even the smallest bit less afraid, the smallest bit less alone.

But that's not the way it is, he reminds himself. *You knew that when you signed up. That's not ever the way it is.*

The Signalman sits at the big bay window of his apartment in the Santa Monica Hills, and he sips his whisky and smokes and watches the sky. Only a few bright stars are visible through the white-orange haze of light pollution. At least that's something. It's surely more than he deserves.

About the Author

Photograph by Kyle Cassidy

CAITLÍN R. KIERNAN is the author of science fiction and dark fantasy works, including ten novels; many comic books; and more than two hundred published short stories, novellas, and vignettes. She is also the author of scientific papers in the field of paleontology. She has won numerous awards, including two World Fantasy Awards, two Bram Stoker Awards, and a James Tiptree, Jr. Award.

TOR·COM

Science fiction. Fantasy. The universe.

And related subjects.

*

More than just a publisher's website, *Tor.com*
is a venue for **original fiction, comics,** and
discussion of the entire field of SF and fantasy,
in all media and from all sources. Visit our site
today—and join the conversation yourself.